The Veil:

Awakening

BY

ZITA GRANT

COPYRIGHT

This is a work of fiction. Names, characters, businesses, places, events and incidents are either the products of the author's imagination or used in a fictitious manner. Any resemblance to actual persons, living or dead, or actual events is purely coincidental.

Text copyright © 2016 by Zita Grant

All rights reserved. Printed in the United States of America.

No part of this book may be reproduced, or stored in a retrieval system, or transmitted in any form or by any means, electronic, mechanical, photocopying, recording, or otherwise, without the express written permission of the publisher.

Published by Zita Grant

Cover design by Jeshart
The first edition

ACKNOWLEDGMENTS

I can hardly say thank you enough Lord for providing the strength to get through this project. Without you, this would never have been possible.

To my family, Imani, Shay and Dwight, your continued encouragement helped me to stay focused. For my late mother Inez, who would have been smiling from ear to ear from this accomplishment, I keep with me your drive and determination to see things through.

Jerry, you have proven to be the embodiment of what God says he will do, he certainly does; words don't do justice to describe my gratitude to and for you.

For all my other friends and colleagues who have been just as excited about this endeavor as I've been "Thank you for believing!"

CHAPTER 1

His eyes darted across the food court, looking for just the right one, so many faces, so many choices.

"That one over there!" The voice said in his head, screaming louder with every word. "Hurry up before they get away, you idiot. No, wait a minute." The voice whispered in a hissing tone,

"That one approaching the side exit, they're perfect."

Quickly as he could move his long legs, the almost zombie-like Richard slithered across the open space, trying to look inconspicuous. Only twenty more feet before the door, he just needed to stay cool; he was almost there.

"Come on, come on, they're getting away. Move faster."

With all the self-control left in his torn mind, Richard kept his right hand from slapping his forehead. He did not want to bring any attention to himself. Just two more steps and he would be home free.

The door was heavy, but he managed to control it from slamming shut once on the other side. No need to alert anyone in the corridor that he was there, just a short distance behind. The light was a bit dimmer and the air was stale. Footsteps up ahead confirmed that his target was still within reach. He could smell her perfume now, sweet like spring flowers on a warm summer's day. Thoughts started to flood his mind of how delicious she would be.

Sweat started to run down the sides of his face, his hands were becoming wet. Licking his lips in anticipation of her body under his control hastened his stride. His steps now gave off a faint echo, loud enough that he feared detection.

"Keep your mind on the task and not on your insignificant desires," growled the voice. "You better remember who's in charge here."

The opening and closing of the exit door ahead made Richard snap out of his daydream. He couldn't let her escape into the open without seeing where she went. Quickly now he walked towards the door. Slowly opening it to sneak a peek at what was on the other side; his target was now approaching a bus stop just to the side the building. Too many people were surrounding her; rage built inside him. Biting his lower lip was all he could do so as not to scream. How desperately he wanted this one. So beautiful and tender, the scent of her perfume still lingered in his nostrils from the heat of the hallway behind him.

"Next time I tell you to do something, you do it!" the voice roared in his head. "I had so many plans for that one, she was just right for the needs inside us"

With hunched over shoulders gazing down at the pavement, Richard walked along the sidewalk heading for the parking lot on the other side of the mall where he'd parked his car. The thought of no restful sleep tonight made him feel even more tired than he already was. The dreams most definitely would be more vivid than before, since the monster that walked around in his head wasn't pacified today. It had been a long time since the last flower petal in the park, when the fear in her eyes made the voice almost sing with pleasure. *How did it even get inside me? What did I do to be paired up with such hatred and vileness?* He thought.

Tears of self-pity started to swell up in his eyes, loathing bubbled in his spirit. Disgusted with himself, he started to form the words to ask the evil to leave him. Before he could even begin to speak a low groan said,

"Don't even think of separating yourself from me. I own you now. Your desire for affirmation and acceptance brought me to you. I like it here and there is nothing you can do to make me leave you."

Without saying a word, Richard continued to walk towards his car. The roar of a truck maneuvering in the parking lot to his left made him think for a second of throwing himself into its path. This way he was sure to be free of this nagging thing. Only a few feet more and it would all be over.

"Oh please go ahead and do it. This way I can choose someone else that is stronger than you to do my bidding. Go on, that's it just a few feet more and you will be mine forever," the voice hissed at him. Urging each footstep with heightening anticipation of the moment Richards's soul would leave its shell.

"Go on do it!"

The sound of the trucks' horn seemed to snap him free from the mental fog. Immediately he stopped moving to stare at the oncoming vehicle. Instinctively he jumped back out of the way. The reality of being forever in the bonds of this monster, made him think soberly for a moment. He decided he must find another way to be free.

The shrieking of Xian's alarm clock made her groan slowly as she rolled over to turn it off. It felt like she just went to sleep. What a set of dreams she had again. Her body felt like it had actually participated in them. The top of her shoulders ached. *A hot shower should do the trick of relaxing those muscles*, she thought.

In a daze, she walked to the bathroom sink, turning on the water and splashing her face, trying to put into perspective the events of her dreams. *Why do I get them now and what do they mean?* She thought to herself staring back at her reflection in the large bathroom mirror.

This time she dreamt of what looked like men, talking to her in a language she could not understand. They seemed just out of phase, as if not really there, not completely solid. She could not make out their facial features, just the outline of their silhouettes. Their voices sounded like flowing waters, strong and constant. Speaking their words in authoritative tones never wavering, they always seemed to be looking directly at her. No eyes to stare back into, yet their presence ways always peaceful, safe.

The cold water on her face made her more awake; the prospect of a good hot shower to ease her aching muscles brought a slight smile to her face. Now even as she stood under the pounding force of the showerheads' spray, their presence seemed to be in the room with her. Replaying the dream over in her mind, she thought she heard someone call her name. It was almost like a faint whisper.

"Xian, Xian" the soft whisper filled the room, making the direction from which it came impossible to tell.

Smiling, she did not make a sound, only spoke within herself,

"Yes, please explain the dream to me so I can understand"

Only the sound of the water hitting her body and the tub echoed in the small room. Her eyes still closed and her mind blank, the dream she had moments ago began to play back in her head like a movie. This time she was watching as if on the sidelines instead of being in it.

She noticed the surroundings of where the event was taking place. The soft sweet voice pointed out significant things to her. Defining each ones relevant meaning, so she would understand the message. Someday she would meet strangers who would show her things to help her understand and use the gifts she had inside her. The things that she hid from everyone, things she feared to share.

"You are at the time when you must learn to use your gifts. You need not be afraid, as The One that gave them to you does not use fear, but love. I will always be with you to show you the way and give you the words to speak. Trust in me and never doubt my direction and you will succeed in your mission," the voice continued as she watched the images move in front of her eyes.

Slowly they faded away and the presence that was just upon her, lifted. The hot water started to become cold, a cue that it was time for Xian's to get out and prepare for her day.

She needed to get moving if she was going to stop at the coffee shop for breakfast before heading to work. Xian's stomach was growling and desired the breakfast special this morning as if she had not eaten in days. With that thought, she hurried to get dressed and within ten minutes was out the door.

Traffic was light, to her surprise. Making it to the coffee shop in record time felt like victory number one for the day. The line inside was not too bad, only four customers ahead. Scanning the menu board to see if anything new was added, she simultaneously reached for her wallet inside her bag. Stepping up to the counter, Xian ordered the special and a small house coffee to go.

After receiving her change, she slowly moved along behind the customers to the pickup counter. Feeling as if from a distant memory, the room began to shift in and out of focus, bits and pieces of it looking oddly familiar, though not just because she had been there so many times before. The tiles on the lower half of the walls along with the bright yellow window treatments, the placement of the furniture were all so familiar. *I saw this place in my dream last night.* Looking at each detail as if for the first time again, in a half daze she collected her order and moved towards the service counter to pick up utensils and sugar for a much-needed cup of coffee.

While taking a sip of the black hot liquid to see if it was sweet enough, she looked to her left to see two men wearing sunglasses like none she had seen before. Something about the frames grabbed her attention.

"You like them?" said one of the men, as she tried to quickly turn away.

"Yes, they have peculiar frames. I've never seen any others like them," said Xian as she reached for some napkins. Turning to look at the men and their sunglasses,

"Where did you get them from?"

They both smiled almost at the same moment, then in unison,

"They came from very far away."

The one closest to her and shorter of the two stepped forward, leaning as if to whisper a secret.

"Would you like to try them on? I must warn you though, they are not ordinary sunglasses, with them on, you are able to see, but we already know that you have the gift, don't we?"

Stunned and gasping for air as if hit hard in the stomach, Xian leaned back a bit before barely getting out,

"Gift, see. I don't..." stopping mid-sentence when she felt the familiar presence come upon her, whispering that it was ok.

"Umm yes, I would like to try them on," she forced the words out of her now dry mouth. Pressure from non-visible strong hands held her shoulders as if bracing her so she would not fall. She slowly put on the pair, eyes kept closed until they were snug on her face. Slowly she opened her eyes surrounded by duplicates. Every building and thing were in full color as she had always seen it but next to each was a reflection like a shadow in a burnt orange and crimson red transparent shade.

Her legs seemed to give for a brief second, but the strength of the hands on her shoulders kept her steady and standing until she gained her footing again. The sharp intake of breath stayed stuck in her chest for what seemed like an eternity; slowly it escaped out through the small opening at the back of her throat.

Her head moved left, up, down, repeating to her right. Everywhere she looked, there were two of everything. The people in the coffee shop were busy doing their own thing. Some had a dark shadow moving in, out and around them. Then there were others that had a white glow emanating from inside them, leaving behind a faint trail of light as they passed by.

Suddenly the dark shadows and glowing lights looked right at Xian. They saw and felt her staring at them. The dark shadows became restless and started to move about frantically. Some seemed to have left the bodies of those they possessed while others that had no bodies, appeared to float towards her. She started to take a step back, when suddenly beings of light materialized standing around her, shielding from the dark shadows. With eyes closed and gasping for air, she pulled the sunglasses off her face and shoved them back at the stranger.

Once her composure was gained, eyes fluttered open as she tried to formulate words as best she could,

"What just happened? What did I just see?"

Ushering her to a nearby table, the men began to answer her question. It seemed like a long time before they spoke. Both looked at her without any facial expression,

just sitting across from her; starring.

"What we speak to you now, no one else can hear us. So, do not be concerned with those around you. To them we are having a casual conversation about nothing in particular."

Xian looked around to see that no one was paying either of them any attention. They all seemed preoccupied with themselves. She looked down at her watch, thinking she did not have much time to chat and if she did, she'd be late for work. *Strange, the second hand's still. I just got a new battery. This thing better not had just died on me.*

"There is nothing wrong with the watch, Xian. Time to us is irrelevant. We are messengers, sent to you to help you prepare for your destiny."

"What destiny? I'm just trying to get to work here. Look, I didn't get much sleep last night and my belly wanted this place's breakfast special with coffee. I need the energy to face the pile of paperwork on my desk today," she said with her head shaking as if to wake up from another dream that felt all too real.

"You are not dreaming, and yes your destiny. Why do you think you have the dreams? Why do your dreams come true if they were only your imagination? How is it that you dreamt of this moment only hours ago and was told of our meeting? Xian's face went pale. "You have been given gifts from on high. Ever since you were a little girl, you were aware of your uniqueness. How you seemed different from those around you. You always received your blessings in a way that would be considered hard by man's standards. Your blessings were indeed hard to get because those that walk in the spiritual realm don't want you to have them. You have been chosen, Xian."

Deafening silence engulfed her. She sat back in her chair, each heartbeat pounding in her ears. Her stomach became a tight knot.

"You have just looked behind the veil that separates this physical existence from that of the spiritual world. The sunglasses you tried on was just a prop to help you see, but you really don't need them. To be able to see behind the veil is also a gift that you must learn to use. After that, you will be able to see at will. You are wondering why you were chosen? Do you even know what your name means?"

Without a sound, she shook her head, eyes never leaving their faces. Her body felt heavy as if being she'd been drugged.

"What you are feeling is the presence of God, he is pouring into you wisdom and understanding of the things you will do in the times ahead. You will be able to see the dark shadows that plague men so that you may help them become free and receive the truth of God. The bright lights you see in and around others are His believers. They already know the truth from Him and like you, are working

to free others, but you are a bit different from the rest."

Silence again, this time to allow all the information just spoken to sink into her. Color slowly coming back into her cheeks, she was now ready for more.

"You have already experienced the touch and voice of God through the Holy Spirit. He is the one that has been directing you thus far. He shall always be with you, we however, have been sent so that you have a tangible body to confirm and communicate with. Another shall come to walk with you on your journey. He will also help you to understand your gifts and to be a more permanent tangible body to communicate with regularly. The things you now know and those that you soon will, cannot be spoken of to just anyone. Look at those around us. Many of their minds would be lost to total confusion if you shared this knowledge with them. They would look at you as if you were crazy."

"How will I know this person, I mean are they just going to appear out of the blue, show up with a business card or something? Just when and where will this meeting take place?" she asked, with fear in her eyes at the thought of now being alone with all this information and no one to hear her rant.

"Don't be afraid, you always have guardians with you even if you can't see them. Honestly, we don't know the time this meeting will happen. Just know that it will."

With her eyes closed and taking long deep breaths, Xian began to calm herself and the fear slowly left.

Xian turned, looking at her surroundings again. Knowing she could no longer deny the unrelenting feelings she's had, she turned back to look at the strangers again, but they were gone. Inside herself she knew it was pointless to try and look for them.

The busy sounds of the coffee shop came rushing into her ears, making her snap back into the present. Looking at her watch while walking out the door, she noticed that only ten minutes had passed since she first entered the building. She felt though as if much more time had passed. Trying not to show how shaken she was by the encounter; she got into her car and headed for work. It was going to be an interesting day. She had to find a way to get through it without daydreaming of all that she had just seen and heard.

God help me, she thought now understanding the dreams and visions she begged to be rid of as a child were preparing her even then for the road she now walked.

The day seemed just like the many before it. Michael sat on the rooftop of the apartments where he lived now for the past 6 years. The morning sun was creeping across the night sky. A new day was dawning and the creatures of the night slowly went into their resting places. The flurry of people below, announced the start of another life-cycle for many as well as the ending for some. Death had come unaware again to thousands on earth; they were warned but thought lightly of the signs. Instead they chose to live their lives without regard only to witness the beginning of eternal torment with the blink of their eyes.

    He too had received a message as he slept as for what seemed like only minutes. Sleep, still a strange experience for him. This flesh body was still taking some getting used to and all that it required. It was time now to go to her. Her journey was started and she must be made ready. Deep inside he hoped she was not going to be that great a challenge. No time to persuade anyone of their destiny, besides his job was to train, not hand hold. The cause was too serious and the price paid too great to deal with any closed minded individuals who could not accept the evidence presented to them. He sighed, praying that his human emotions that came with this suit of flesh were unjustified.

    Daylight now flooded the entire horizon; time to go to work. He knew that he had until sunset to find her. After that, she would be confused by the attacks that were already making moves towards her. The veil for her had been removed. She could see every wicked thing out there and they knew it, not a good thing if unprepared. Ready or not her life certainly had changed. By this time of morning she was sure to be on her way to work. In another hour or so, she would be buried in her daily routine. He thought he'd better appear clean shaven and wear something other than all black clothes, no need to look so gloomy. Michael made his way back down the staircase to his apartment, second guessing why he was even bothering to change his appearance; not like it really mattered in the scheme of things anyways. Then he remembered his instructions, to appeal to her every emotion, as she is well in tuned to all of hers. Her trust must be gained at first contact. No time to play cat and mouse, or go against the grain. *Whatever it takes* he thought.

His apartment was sparsely decorated since he really didn't require much and not like this was a permanent gig. There was a single bed in the farthest corner from the door with a nightstand and a lamp. In the center of the room a small three-piece table and chair set. Along the large double window was a worn sofa. The interior screamed temporary, definitely no long-term attachment. It took only a few minutes for him get ready. Speed was something he had, naturally. Time was something he disliked to waste.

Hopefully her morning chat went well and she's open to taking the next step he thought as he stepped out onto the streets sidewalk. Just two blocks ahead was where she worked. He could just make out the roof of the building as he weaved through pedestrians still shuffling about trying to get where ever it was they were in such a hurry to get to. Eyes scoured the sky, nothing but clouds. No one seemed to be paying him any particular interest either as he made his way. He didn't know whether to be glad or concerned with that observation, but then again, none of the others knew she was his assignment; yet.

The glass doors to the office building seemed to effortlessly glide open as he approached them. It was as if time slowed down, the closer he got to her. Whether it was great timing or just the perfect opportunity, either way, the open doors of the empty elevator beckoned to him. With the flick of his wrist, the elevator camera lost its focus. He decided his outfit still wasn't going to make that good an impression on her. Looking at his reflection in the elevator doors, he shrugged his shoulders in defeat looking at his dark rugged clothes and wild tossed hair falling just below his shoulders. Suddenly he was changed into a business suit and neatly slicked back locks. Now with a briefcase in hand he flicked his wrist again to reset the camera while the elevator doors opened onto the twenty-first floor. Immediately, the buzz of the open space hit his ears. Workers scurried about getting on with their days assignments. Some on the phone, others chatting, while a melody of keyboard strokes played in the background.

With the blink of his eyes, he tuned out every sound. Slowly walking down the center aisle of cubicles, he listened for the voice of her spirit. Each step made it clearer, the soft words of prayer she repeated. Something had her spooked; she kept calling out to God for help. To his left he caught the white light of her aura. Busily she typed on her computer, whilst talking on the phone. Suddenly she stopped and looked right up at him. Her gaze seemingly looked straight through his disguise.

"Ernie, I'm gonna' have to call you back. Umm I just got a visitor, umm ok!" she spoke into the phone.

Eyes never leaving him, she put down the handset and stood up, straitening her clothes as she did. With her head slightly tilted to the left she said,

"Hello Xian Reed, can I help you?"

"It is I, who came to help you, Xian," said Michael in a firm low tone, "my name is Michael, the help you requested."

Xian's face became flushed; she was a bit confused by the statement. Her mind sorting at light speed through her thoughts, wondering what help she requested. She didn't remember asking her boss for any, although she could use it. She thought it best to play along and get all she could while the chance lasted.

"Ah, did Mr. Fredrick request you from the Temp Pool for me?"

With a slight smile, Michael realized she hadn't uncovered who he really was, even though the connection she made with her eyes was strong enough to do so; if she knew how to look.

"Actually no, I'm the help you asked for earlier this morning. The coffee shop, remember?" he said tilting his head slightly to the side to mimic her.

As if all the breath had been knocked out of her for the millionth time in one morning, Xian felt her legs get weak. She reached for her desk to balance herself. Wide eyed she stared at the image before her, mind racing, wondering if this too was really happening. Color slowly returned to her face as she swallowed hard to moisten her dry throat.

"You," she managed to blurt out, "how, why, wait I mean I know why but kinda' fast don't you think?"

"You have been chosen, remember?"

"Chosen? Here we go again, I mean seriously for what? Like why me? Why am I being singled out?"

With a plastic smiling Michael, reached out to help her sit down. She appeared lost to all that had happened so far. *This one needs a lot of coaching; great! There is such little time and this here baby still doesn't know how to crawl.*

CHAPTER 2

Richard had only about five hours left to sleep. The nightmares at first made him toss and turn. Only out of share exhaustion, was he able to drift off into a black void; no sound, no pictures, just darkness. This was a welcomed paradise, after the long day he had. The time to go back to work would fast approach and he had to be able to shift gears before stepping back into the office. No one could ever find out about his secret, he had to keep it locked up until he found a way to get rid of it once and for all. *Sleep, sweet sleep,* he thought as he curled up in bed. The light still on in the room helped Richard to not feel so alone, offering a little sense of comfort to his tormented existence.

Yes go to sleep, the voice thought to himself, *you will need all your energy. We have much work to do before your meaningless life is ended.*

As he slept, Richard started to dream of his childhood. He must have been about eight years old, was playing with his toy train set while his parents argued again in the bedroom next to his. Their voices pierced through the walls, sounding as though they were standing right next to him.

Louder and louder the sounds grew; then the smashing of furniture began. Screams and curses yelled back and forth. To help drown out the sounds, Richard turned on the radio. The heavy metal music screamed from the speakers of the small box radio. Turning the volume as loud as possible, he rocked back and forth as he sat on the floor watching his train go around the tracks. Around and around it went. Almost hypnotizing him along with the music.

How he longed to get away from this house of hatred. He decided to grow up and leave and never to see either one of them again. If only he could escape them now, just even for a little while. Anything anywhere would be better than this. Again he began to rock back and forth, eyes fixed to the train until they focused on nothing.

Over the sound waves of music filling his room, he thought he heard his name being called. Thinking it was just one of his parents, he ignored it. Again his name rang out but this time he realized it wasn't either of them. As he stared into the void that once was the center of his train track, he saw a hand reaching for him.

"Take my hand. Let me show you a peaceful place where you can have anything you want. I can take you away from all the shouting and screams," said the voice in a calm tone, coaxing him to come closer.

"That's it, just take my hand. We can be friends forever."

The fighting seemed to be getting worse between his parents. Wanting to just be free of them, Richard grabbed the hand and before he could blink was pulled into the void. Weightlessness surrounded his body. He felt as if he was floating. Thinking this must be a dream, he decided to enjoy the diversion. The sound of what he thought was wind blowing in trees slowly filled his ears. As his vision focused on the images that began to come into view, a sickening feeling crept up the back of his throat.

With eyes widening, he saw that the source of the sound was not tree leaves blowing in the wind, but that of people crying and struggling to climb over each other. They seemed to be reaching for an opening in the black sky. Teeth grinding in every mouth, bodies covered in cuts and bruises. Thier hands got closer, coming to him, then he understood. This was the place his parents wished each other would go almost every day. Rising heat laced with the scent of sulfur and specs of ash filled the air; torment everywhere; hell.

In a flash the images changed, he was suddenly sitting on a beautiful patch of deep green grass. A refreshing waterfall seemingly reaching all the way to the black sky was just to the edge of it, straight ahead. The water looked so inviting and Richard could imagine how great it would feel to wash away the screams and lonely feelings his parents filled his mind and heart with. Slowly he walked towards the water's edge and just before he could test it with his feet, a sweet sounding voice directly behind him said,

"Welcome home Richard. Here is where you can escape all the pain you feel anytime you wish. Isn't it beautiful, peaceful?"

"Yes it is," Richard choked out. "Ah what though were all those people crying about earlier and why was it so hot and smelly?"

By this time he was face to face with the source of the voice. It was a man, he thought, but he didn't really seem to be like all the others Richard had ever seen. His hands looked soft like his mothers, face smooth like hers too; a smooth pasty color. This guy needed to get more sun, he thought. His eyes weren't green, blue or brown; they looked like a mixture of all with red flecks flashing at times. Smiling at Richard now, the man took his right hand and led him into the water, stopping under the waterfall.

Cool refreshing water fell on them both. Richard closed his eyes and let it wash away every thought and memory of his turbulent childhood.

"Isn't this wonderful Richard? You can feel this way anytime you like, you know."

"How do I get back here when I want to return?"

"Easy, just call my name and close your eyes. I'll come right away and bring you here."

Such a nice person this man is. Wait, I don't even know his name, how will I call him.

"But I don't even know your name?"

"You can call me Buddy."

Richard smiled as he thought of having a special savior who would come and rescue him from his miserable home whenever he needed. Peace and joy seemed to come over him for hours. Suddenly the sound of his room door flying open shattered the experience. Standing now just behind him was his mother, trying to wipe the tears away from her swollen eyes and keep her voice steady as she spoke.

"Come on baby let's get you ready for bed, huh?"

"Ok mom," he blurted out.

Trying to lick his lips and create saliva, he rubbed his throat reaching for the glass of water on his nightstand, drinking it as if it was his first glass of the day; he choked after the first gulp.

"You okay baby. Just take your time and drink slower."

Nodding he looked up and smiled, trying to outdo her strained one. She kissed his forehead rearranging his hair with her fingers. Maybe she thought this made him forget the fights, he knew she hurt inside and felt trapped.

"Someday soon, everything will be better baby, you'll see. Daddy just had a bad day that's all."

It was like a broken record. She'd make the same excuses and try to sing him to sleep, all the while fighting back tears and trying to mask the terror in her eyes.

"Yeah someday mom, we'll be happy again and maybe we can start taking family day trips like we used to."

Family day trips were the best. They would pick a place in the city to visit and spend the day exploring, enjoying new foods and each other's company. That stopped though after dad lost his job and mom couldn't bring in enough money to help cover all the bills. It was the beginning of two years of fights and bad days for not just dad, but everyone. He hoped someday would come soon because each morning felt like a repeat of the one before.

A piercing riff of electric guitar music sliced through the air from the radio alarm next to the bed. Richard frantically reached for the snooze button; he couldn't believe it was morning already. He still needed more sleep, but this morning he had a deadline to meet at work and he was already behind schedule. With all the energy he could muster, he dragged into the bathroom to get changed. Looking at his reflection in the mirror, he definitely needed some major grooming today. The stubbles on his jawline and chin, not to mention the dark circles under his bloodshot eyes meant at least an extra twenty minutes in the bathroom this morning.

About ten blocks away Xian was taking a hard hot shower. The forceful water on the back of her neck seemed to pound new energy into her body. She felt unusually tired this morning, as if she hardly got any rest last night. *Wait, last night, the last thing I remember was being at work and that fine as all outdoors stranger. How did I get here in my shower? Where did the last half a day go? What's happening to me?* She screamed in her head.

Noting that the water was real and that she was awake, she stepped out of the shower, reaching for her cell phone to check the date and time. With a panic stare, it was the next morning as she feared. Meaning she had definitely lost time; a lot of it. After taking several deep breaths, she got dressed while trying to piece together the events of yesterday, leading up to this moment. Yet all she could think of was the stranger. *He must have something to do with what's happening to me. He mentioned that I was chosen but he* never said what fort. At least I don't think he did and what was his name again?

    Slowly a burning itching sensation started to intensify just on her right shoulder; reaching for it, her fingers touched what felt like a scar. She twisted her body to get a better look in the mirror. Some sort of symbol marked her skin in what looked like red ink. A tattoo, she would never get one. *What did that bastard do to me and did he, did we?* she thought shaking her head hoping she didn't get slipped some date rape drug.

    "Okay," she said out loud while putting on her shoes, "get a grip and pull yourself together, finished getting dressed and go to work. That guy has to be there somewhere and when you find him he better have some answers or you go straight to the police."

    Feeling a bit more grounded, she hurried out the door and made a mental note to stop for breakfast at her favorite coffee shop. *Yeah maybe just for coffee and at all cost avoid interacting with strangers today*. Her stomach was in no mood for food right now.

    Within an hour Xian was walking up to her office building coffee long done, the tight knot in her stomach only seemed to get tighter with each step. Thoughts racing she didn't even notice that the bright sunny day had suddenly become overcast and gray. With just one roar of thunder, rain began to pound the earth as if a faucet was fully opened; everyone started to scurry into nearby buildings for shelter, yet as they began to run, instead of moving faster they started to slow down. Everything around her slowed down even the falling rain drops. Then he called her given names,

"Xian Nikamah," in what sounded like many voices roaring over what should be the loud sound of the thunderous rain which by now had stopped falling all around her.

Feeling like she was in a movie straight out of Sci-Fi, she tried to get a fix on where the voices were coming from but couldn't, then she heard her name again, only louder, closer. This time it was coming from right in front of her, but no one was there. Like mist being cut by an object a figure formed before her, shaped by the rain drops. It was him, that heart stopping long dark haired helper. This time dressed in all white, even his hair was void of color, but his eyes were blue like the varying lighter shades of the beaches she would retreat to when she was younger. He reached for her arm leading her away from the office building, everything around them still moved in slow motion. Her heart was starting to really race now and wide-eyed she tried to make sense of it all, still struggling with the notion that it was really happening. After just the blink of her eyes, they were no longer down on the street level but were now standing high above the city on a rooftop and the rain cloud slowly drifted away, letting the sunshine begin to dry up the drenched ground.

"You have many questions, I know and I have your answers but first I need to lay a little foundation for them to stand on. I am Michael the one sent to guide and teach you about your destiny."

Xian heard the words but they were not sinking in. Nothing was making any sense and how did they get on top of a roof, they were just walking on the sidewalk in the rain. The feeling of a firm grip on her arms and the back and forth motion of her head, made her focus on his face and words more.

"Are you listening to me?" He asked in a low calm tone. This time his voice was only of one person. He could see how confused she was and hear here heart racing. Slowly her breathing became more regular as she began to focus more on their surroundings. As calm as she could, Xian asked if she was dreaming and the knot in her stomach squeezed painfully tighter as he shook his head, no.

"Look around you. Do you see the once hidden images that exist in your world?"

Xian slowly gazed and saw what looked like people following others around, but they looked deformed somehow. It was difficult to see from so high up but when she looked up in the clouds, she saw winged, human-like looking creatures flying while others were in a sitting position, sitting on nothing, just hovering way up in the air. Michael held her steady as she faulted, her legs were buckling and then she grabbed her stomach while squeezing her eyes close tight. He knew she now saw everything behind the veil that keeps most oblivious to what is really happening around them.

"Do you know the meaning of your name?" after she shook her head he continued, "it means Sword of Vengeance, but you may be wondering whose sword and whose vengeance you are. You can no longer deny or run from your gift Xian, everything has a purpose and The Almighty has one just for you. You are His Sword and Vengeance on the fallen that work to destroy His creation; mankind. Now that you can see behind the veil they know it; you'll be watched even more."

At the same time Michael had called out Xian's given names, the sound pierced the ears of everything old, held sacred, cursed and damned. The feared moment had come for many and longed for by others, which would release His wrath, and the strongholds of Satan's minions would be loosening. Every evil thing shuddered in fear of what was coming their way. This one would awaken many others and the charades that have carried on throughout time would no longer keep mankind blind to the truth. Thousands scurried around as if in a daze, wondering where to hide now that the Sword of Vengeance's eyes had been opened. They knew that many of them would be sent to the pit and consumed by fire way before they desired, only Master can protect them now; *must tell him* was the consuming thought that rang through them all.

    Watching from above the earth's stratosphere, Satan saw his legions becoming restless. He too heard Michaels voice and the name he spoke. *At last, some real action is about to take place with an impressive opponent.* Michael was very skilled in battle and would no doubt train this puny monkey to certainly put a damper on his plans and delay progress in taking all the souls he could. *No matter though just like every other who has tried, this one to shall fall and all of Gods precious, loved monkeys will worship me. I will soon be just like The Most High, just as I planned when once living in Heaven. What could be so special about this one, no one is a match for me,"* Satan thought as he stretched his neck and squared his shoulders looking down at the chaos below, loving every minute of it.

    "Master, Master, we have trouble. Michael has helped the Sword of Vengeance to see beyond the veil.

They will be coming for us. What shall we do Master?" said a short demon, head down cowering at Satan's feet.

"Get up you fool. You and your brothers have nothing to fear, this one is of no consequence to our plans. We still rule this world and all in it."

As if walking to the edge of a high cliff, Satan walked along the air and looked down more intently focusing on the area where Xian and Michael were. With hands clasped behind his back he decided to summon his team to advise they contemplate new strategies in order take on whatever surprises lay ahead. He called to his generals Azazel, Beelzebub, Carreau, Dagon, Meresin and Verrine. Within an instant they were beside him, heads bowed awaiting his permission to straighten. He looked at each formulating ways for them to guard against the loss of his hold on mankind from Xian in the times ahead and how to destroy her permanently.

They each had an important stronghold over the earth and mankind. Azazel's was the deserts and dry places. Beelzebub was the prince of his minions. Carreau hardened the hearts of men. Dagon was the prince of the depths and wet places whose symbolism was evident in many churches. Meresin was the prince of the air who controlled the thunder and lightning with the ability to cause fire and plagues. While Verrine tempted man with impatience and could motivate them to action, *what a team!*

"With my victory of destroying Adam and Eve's life in the Garden of Eden, this day was long known to come. His Sword of Vengeance has awakened who precedes the return of Christ to this wretched paradise; we must be ready. Each of you knows your strengths, use them to destroy this puny monkey so we can get on with our soul gathering.

They each remained with heads bowed, thinking to themselves how best to prepare for the days ahead. Neither wanted to fail Satan or appear weak in front of the other. No one wanted to be on the receiving end of his wrath. For as beautiful as he appears, Satan's heart is as steel; hard and cold. He has proven to let nothing stand in his way of winning this war of souls. With each one their minions take, his eyes seem to burn brighter.

Sensing their restlessness, Satan turned to face them. A mischievous grin on his lips, he said,

"Come on now, smile. Don't look so concerned. Surely we can destroy this female, can't we?"

In unison they all shouted a roaring yes while bowing their heads even lower. Neither of them wanted to catch the gaze of Satan, fearing any hint of doubt showing in their eyes. His cruelty knew no bounds. Satan stared at them bowing for a brief moment, and then focused his gaze beyond their bent backs. He tried to figure out how Xian would be used in this battle. What special abilities did she have over the others he wondered? Whatever they were, he'd be ready. This city was his. His stronghold was mighty and grew stronger each day. Greed and lust for power perfumed its air. The mindless people were so wrapped up in chasing success and believing any doctrine spoken only made his job easier. This day dawned the beginning of a change, one he planned to go in his favor.

CHAPTER 3

Richard stood inside the break room at work lazily stirring sugar into his cup of coffee. It was his third for the morning and there was still another hour to go before lunch. He signed deeply and tried to focus on the project he had to complete before the end of the day. Working at the ad agency did have its perks of half wall windows which took advantage of natural light. It also gave great city views and visual distractions needed when staring at a computer screen most of the day. With shoulders squared he walked back towards his desk. Everyone worked in a large open area with private cubicles that had adjustable walls. His were mostly all the way up which helped him focus. Yet sometimes he would lower them near the end of the day. This was mostly to observe his co-workers, many who were clueless to the man behind the painted on smile.

Secretly he had observed them all, followed them covertly on most social media sites and picked ones he wanted to befriend and date. They didn't know since he barely spoke to them outside of work related conversations. However, lately he couldn't help himself with probing them for more social information; what their plans were for after work, the upcoming weekend, holiday. Buddy's voice kept pushing him to make small conversations with practically anyone. He slowly learned how to pick anything of common interest related to work as an opener then branch off into personal thoughts on career and dreams. Subtle hints were made in these conversations, playing upon the desires others had. Each hint watering the seeds of doubt, pride, self-loathing, and lust. Before they knew it, depression was creeping its way into their minds and hearts. Buddy had yet again cultivated the perfect mindset for him to take over their will power.

    Richard began to realize that Buddy wanted to take away the hope of people and in their despair give them a seemingly restful place, just as he did him as a young boy. Every time he sees the light fade from people's eyes he spoke with, a part of him aches. How he fights with wanting someone to rescue him and take away the pain, yet this is quickly pushed down with the ever present Buddy whispering in his ears.

    He shook his head as if to rearrange the web of thoughts. Focusing on the computer screen at his desk, he proceeded to work on finishing the ad presentation his boss was pestering him for. Deciding he would work through lunch and be done sooner, he took a sip of coffee and leaned closer to the screen. A light sounding female's voice broke his concentration as it drifted over his right shoulder.

"Hi Richard, do you have the proofs for the Quang Corp by chance?"

It was Jenny from the accounts services department. She was a rather skinny, pale skinned young woman with red hair and several freckles that dotted her face and chest. Her smile was infectious and her eyes were always bright. Richard liked the ease she had interacting with others, which made her so good at her job. Hers was one of the more successful portfolios the company had lately and Jenny knew just how to get things done, her way. Her most used tactic was indirect manipulation. Many didn't really notice since it was overshadowed by her playful body language, the tone of voice, often placed cluelessness and again, infectious smile. Always the smart and sexy dresser, she used everything she had to distract you from her main objective. Getting things her way, done on her schedule, period. Buddy had long tipped him to her motives but he found her almost irresistible.

"Ah yes I do," Richard managed to get out after swallowing the hot liquid from his coffee cup, trying to not smack so much in attempts to cool his tongue.

He turned his chair to his left and reached over to pick up a binder on his desk. Spinning around to face her, he stood up handing the binder to Jenny. Before he could even think of words to say, sounds were coming out of his mouth.

"Here you go. Are they coming in to look them over?"

"Yes this afternoon. Thanks for rushing this for me, I know you're swamped. I owe you one," Jenny replied smiling with body getting ready to pivot and walk away.

"Ah yes about that one you owe me. You can settle it over a drink or bite to eat after work. How about tomorrow? You can let me know how today's meeting goes with Quang Corp."

With a bit of shock on her face, Jenny stopped dead in her tracks. She hadn't really expected him to collect. It was something she said just to brush him off. Mentally she was in a panic trying to figure out how to get out of actually paying back the favor. Nothing was coming to her and she needed to end the awkward silence that was engulfing them. After another ten seconds she still had nothing. With all the perkiness she could muster, her mouth blurted out,

"Sure okay, tomorrow after work we can go check out the new menu items at Tequila Grill. I heard they have some really tasty additions. Hmm say around six thirty?"

"No tomorrow won't do, let's make it tonight say around the same time. I want an instant return for my favor. I will wait for you out in the lobby."

With wide eyes and a slight gasp, Jenny looked at Richard in disbelief of his boldness. He certainly was turning out to be more than the quiet shy guy.

As if realizing she was caught off guard, with a clearing of her throat and toss of hair she slightly nodded and uttered,

"Yes sure."

Richard could hardly believe what had just happened. Not only did he ask a girl out on a date, she actually accepted. With all the confidence he could pull out of his chest, he casually shifted all his weight on his left leg, hands shoved in his pant pockets and nodded with a smile. Watching Jenny walk away, he felt a sudden boost of pride.

"You don't really think that was all your doing, do you?" Buddy's voice said.

Like a reaction to a punch in the stomach, Richard sank down into his desk chair. His face felt hot with rising anger.

"Of course it was all me," he mumbled. "I was the one doing all the talking and eye contact."

The sound of an increasingly louder chuckle filled his head. Then there was a sudden silence which made Richards' shoulders relax, and drop. When he though Buddy had left him, his firm voice said,

"Never be fooled dear boy. All the words you say are mine! I own you and control every little smile, hand gesture and heart beat your body does. I am always with you. You belong to me! Come on now, let's not dilly dally, you've got to finish this project so you don't work late. I have something for you to do tonight."

Richard swallowed hard and rubbed his temples. All he had initially planned to do tonight was sleep. He desperately wanted just to curl up in his bed and think or hear nothing. Tonight seemed like a good time to break open the seal on the sleep aid pills he bought. A slow smile crossed his face as he remembered his plan to quiet Buddy's voice if only for a night, or two. *Ah, looks like that plan will have to wait at least for one more night.*

Six thirty seemed to come faster than Richard expected, but then again he had been practically glued to his desk finishing up his workload. Pushing away from his keyboard he leaned back in his chair and stretched his arms. Cracking sounds came from them and his neck. He felt exhausted. Wishing for a hot shower and his bed, he momentarily closed his eyes. With deep breaths he felt his body begin to relax. The sounds of the office faded away and his mind became blank. After what felt like several minutes he slowly opened his eyes and checked the time. It had only been thirty seconds. Smiling to himself he began to draft the email to his boss and attach his files. It was six fifteen, just enough time left to wrap up his day and splash some cold water on his face to disguise his tiredness.

Six twenty-nine and Jenny stood near the office entrance inside the lobby area. Still as a statue with eyes fixed on the street outside she waited for Richard. Something about him was different lately.
Today his directness took her by surprise. *When did he grow a pair?* It was the first time in what seemed like forever, anyone had knocked her off balance. The look in his eyes gripped her in a strange way. The deepest part of her being stirred with each moment she gazed into them; something was staring back, familiar yet not fully understood. Something recognizable; someone!

The elevator doors opened. A rush of people made their way towards her. Sidestepping she searched the faces for Richard's. Every other head bopping and weaving revealed a slight glimpse of him as he brought up the rear. Then he was standing in front of her. His eyes sparkled. A slight smirk lingered at the corners of his mouth. He stood straight with pushed out chest almost looking at her in a condescending way. Without saying a word, he motioned with his right hand to walk toward the entrance. Wait a minute; she recognized that look, the body language. It was the same that reflected when she looked in the mirror most of the time. Could he also be like her? Could he be special, knowing things, seeing things? Swallowing hard she smiled and followed Richard's lead out onto the busy sidewalk.

The distance to Tequila Grill was literally six doors down from their office. No words were exchanged as each tried to make sense of what was happening between them. Soon upon entering the establishment, they were seated in a booth near the back of the restaurant. It was just far enough from the loud voices of the happy hour crowd near the bar for them to have a private conversation. The lighting was not too bright, which Richard was grateful for since he knew his eyes would soon show signs of sleep deprivation once the effects of the cold water he splashed on wore off.

After their drinks were served and orders were taken, Richard leaned back into the booth and looking straight into Jenny's eyes asked,

"So how long has it been since you've heard his voice?"

With rapid eye blinks Jenny tried not to choke on a mouthful of soda. She purposely didn't order any alcohol; she wanted to be fully alert tonight. Had to know what Richard was up to, what he really wanted from her.

"What umm I don't understand your question?"

"Oh come now. We both know fully well what the question is referring to. I can see it in your eyes, your body language."

"I haven't the faintest idea what you're talking about. If you want to know something, just ask plainly."

"Very well," Richard said, this time in a firm deep voice, the sound of which made Jenny's stomach lurch.

"Do you hear the voice when you're pretty much alone, or does it speak to you at any given time?"

Jenny's mind was racing for an answer at this point. One that wouldn't give away too much yet opened the door to probing him more for why he wanted to know.

With a forced laugh she shuffled in her seat. Slowly twirling the straw in her glass and without looking up said,

"Don't we all hear voices? I mean doesn't everyone talk to themselves?"

"Yes I guess we all talk to ourselves from time to time. That however, is not what I meant and you know it."

At this point the waiter brought their food. Glad of the interruption and hoping to change the direction of their conversation, Jenny made a comment as to how delicious everything looked. Richard leaned forward to show interest and agreed. Still he noticed how her hand shook slightly when reaching for her fork and napkin. She was unsettled. Buddy was making her nervous with his probing. Now Richard himself was becoming curious as to just how and why she heard Buddy's voice. He wondered if he was known as Buddy to her or by some other name. They ate in silence for some time, only to periodically smile at each other while chewing their food. Jenny had become relaxed.

"Mention summer camp to her, how you never had a chance to go but longed to whenever the boys in school talked about all the hot girls they hooked up with there. Ask her if she ever had a red swimsuit," Buddy whispered in Richard's ears.

Richard looked puzzled about the red swimsuit comment. Then figured it must hold some significance to her breaking moment when Buddy became real to her.

Slowly he drank his fruit punch. With patience he waited for her to finish swallowing her mouthful of food. Then when she looked up at him he hit her with the words.

"Tell me about summer camp and the cute red swimsuit. I'm sure you were the envy of every girl there and dream of all the adolescent boys."

As if she was suddenly sitting there naked, Jenny's hands instinctively moved to cover herself; the movement made Richard's eyebrows rise slightly and he felt the heat growing in his pants. He tried to slow his racing heartbeat as he imagined her naked in front of him. Her voice pulled him back from his thoughts.

"Huh, summer camp, red swimsuit?" Jenny stuttered. Her head felt light, the food she so much enjoyed eating was now threatening to come back up and spew all over the table. What did this fool know about her past, but more importantly how did he know was all she could think.

"Why would you ask me about such particular childhood events? And how do you know about my summer camp days or what swimsuits I owned?"

She sat there as pale as a ghost. All her color had drained from her face. Even her freckles seemed lighter. With eyes glassed over with tears she starred back at Richard. He saw the fear creeping on her face. He felt her pain as he reached for her hand. Gently he patted it and gave as reassuring a smile as possible. Then softly he said,

"I know because the voice speaks to me also. He tells me things about people I could never have known. Your secrets are safe with me Jenny. You are safe with me."

Realizing that neither of them would be able to eat anymore, with his free right hand he signaled to the waiter for the check. As Jenny gathered herself, Richard paid the waiter and then stood next to her offering his hand to help her up. Now a bit more collected, she took it and they left the restaurant hand in hand. Something felt protective of the way he held onto her. For a brief moment she let herself feel his touch. Even when the loud street sounds jolted her back to reality, he didn't let her hand go, even when she tried to wiggle free. They walked back to their office parking garage and once next to her car, he gently cupped her face and kissed her. Jenny felt like she was watching it all take place outside her body. Before she realized what was going on, her hands were turning her steering wheel and she was driving out of the garage into the evening traffic.

"What just happened," she yelled to herself in the car while at a red light.

The long forgotten snickering sound from her childhood filled her ears. A sound she'd tried so hard to quench.

"Why was it back now? How did it get back? Richard. What did he know of this torment? Can he help me be rid of it once and for all?" she whispered as she began to drive along in the flow of traffic.

Peering down from the sky, Satan looked about the Earth for easy targets whose souls he could snatch. Calculatingly, with clasped hands rubbing the tip of his nose, he decided which of his generals he would use to reap the fresh harvest of those completely indulged in selfish ambition. Every day, thousands upon thousands drew closer to him than they realized; compromising their selves for earthly gain. He smiled at the thought of his increasing power. The more of them he controlled, the more fighting power he had over those that served against his will. Foolish puppets, didn't they know how difficult it was to be rid of him. He ruled the air; he is the Prince of the Air. They all had to go through him to reach God. At least it made the time go by, all of their whining and denials. Secretly he enjoyed it, the cat and mouse games they played. Now stroking his left temple he thought of Xian. She could prove to be a pain if she measured up to expectations.

With the call of Verrine's name, Satan summoned him to his side. Within moments he stood beside him, head bowed awaiting permission to speak or move.

"You will oversee my first strike against Xian Verrine. I want you to temp her, make her feel ready to take on my minions. Increase her impatience to learn all that Michael has to teach her."

"Yes my lord, as you wish."

"I want her full of herself to the point she feels Michael's warnings are not important and are for weaklings. Make her vulnerable."

"Yes my lord, it shall be done," said Verrine before he left Satan's side. He felt honored to be the first one used and promised to his-self he wouldn't fail. He would surely gain more favor from his lord when he accomplished his mission. More power was going to be his and Xian would be the means it came through.

He would watch her every move. See what her weaknesses really were. Michael was known to have a very strong hold on those he mentored. No one could quite figure out just how he did it. What secret leverage did he use on them? Regardless, Verrine was sure he would crack that hold and push a wedge between him and Xian. With focused eyes and a slight smile, he flew over the city, circling the areas she frequented. A faint dark mist rose from just to his right. As he descended to perch on the roof of a tall building's ledge, he could see thousands of minions gathering around a particular building. The closer he flew towards them, he was able to to see what they intently moved towards. Two figures stood on the roof; it was Michael and Xian. Quickly he hid behind a gargoyle statue sitting menacingly at the corner of the building adjacent to where the action was. Happy that he wasn't spotted by Michael, he made his was down the side of the building, carefully staying just out of sight from those piercing eyes.

Well she didn't faint which is a good thing, Michael thought as he watched Xian begin to breathe normally, *she didn't appear completely freaked out by what just took place. Maybe she is really ready to accept her fate.* Just over her left shoulder, Michael noticed movement. Movement no normal human could do. The sun rays that flashed off its surface proved it most likely was a fallen one in full armor; a general. Not surprised by the speed Satan took to send one of his hounds, Michael pretended not to notice. He patiently waited for a few more moments to catch a glimpse of their new stalker. He began to count down from five in his head. By the time he got to one, a face peered around the side of a building.

"Got you," he whispered, *Verrine,* of course he thought. *Who else would be so sneaky?*

"So you're going to fill her head with nonsense and make her think I'm of no importance," he mumbled to himself, "same tricks just a different target, how predictable you all have become." Michael mused as he began to show the slightest smile.

Xian caught it. An ever so slight upward turn of his lips, slow bowing of his head.

"Why the smile," she asked with a hint of surprise in her voice.

"Nothing to worry your head about, we have lots to do. Let's get going," he said as he guided her toward the stairwell.

"I don't remember taking the stairs to get up here. Just how did we get up here?"

"Like this," replied Michael as he held her close to him while they did what her mind could best describe as floating downward but only at a faster pace. Within seconds they were standing on the street below. Xian being not too fond of heights didn't get that stomach flipping sensation though as then traveled. With questioning eyes she asked him why not.

"It's because I experience time and space differently from you. Since we were physically connected, so did you. The movement doesn't have the same sensations as you would have expected while changing heights."

The expression on her face made him add,

"Don't even think of achieving this yourself. Remember you and I are different. This is not something you can do in that body. Do you understand me?"

He was now holding her by the shoulders, looking at her with the most serious expression. His eye color was now the darkest brown she had ever seen. Silently she nodded, body stiffening under his gaze. When his grip relaxed, so did she. For all the tough vibes he gave off, she could sense he had a lot of passion. She would make a mental note to stay on his good side. At this closeness Xian was able to take a good look at him. He was handsome, no doubt about it. He wasn't big and muscular, but lean and toned. Figuring he didn't need muscle mass as human men, what he did appear to have must make him quite the opponent. She had been observing his movements, always purposeful; sure. He made her feel safer than anyone ever had. She felt she could tell him about things no one else would ever understand.

Sensing her watching him as they continued to walk along the sidewalk, he took her hand turning her to face him. Slowly he sighed. Xian's face began to blush as if she had been caught stealing something. No matter how she tried to stop looking into his eyes, she couldn't. Almost paralyzed by their closeness she heard him telling her to breathe. Why did she lose it whenever he was around she wondered.

"We are not going to have that kind of relationship Xian. My duty is to teach you and help you in this fight. This face you fantasize over is not my own. It is but a reflection of someone I came across. These are his eyes you look at, his smile you see. However, the actions are all mine. It is my essence that connects with that part of you

God controls. We were made by the same creator. Do you understand me?"

"Yes," she said with slight disappointment on her face.

"Don't worry; someday there will be a time in your life for love."

"There will? Will he understand all this veil stuff or is that a secret I'll have to keep from him?"

"The answer will be made clear to you when necessary, but that is for another time. Right now you have to train. What you saw is only a fraction of what is out there. You have to be ready to fight and not by the ways you're thinking."

Xian couldn't imagine any human man being more important to her than Michael. He was a strength she realized was so vacant from her life until now. Even if this love she would have shared anything resembling Michael, they were not the same. A handsome face was not what she needed. She needed strength, trust. Deciding to push the love thoughts out of her head for now, she focused on preparing for whatever was coming. Regardless of what this training involved, she was determined to master it. No longer would she suffer in silence, finding herself sometimes afraid to really live. If there was a way to fight back, she was all in. Noticing her head was high and stride more confident, he said without looking at her,

"I will be with you as long as you need me Xian. You can trust in this. I know trust has been a great issue for you. So many have not held their end of the bargain in your life, but I will not desert you."

She smiled, her heart felt light and full of joy. People passing by were smiling as they looked in their direction. The women particularly were checking Michael out, who just kept looking straight ahead. *Did he not desire them? Did he desire anything?* As if he heard her thoughts he answered,

"If you saw them the way I do, you wouldn't give them any attention either. Yes I have desires, but not of anything in this world."

Nodding Xian continued to walk with him for a few more blocks. Rounding a corner, they arrived at a small store. A bell chimed as Michael opened the door, revealing the interior representing a hodgepodge of almost anything imaginable. There were showcases filled with what looked like antiques; plaques and artwork hung along the wall behind a long counter on one side of the store. Slowly the sound of the outside faded away as the front door closed behind them, resulting in a deadly silence as if they were in a vacuum.

A short bald man came out of the back and walked up to the counter where they stood. His gaze was fixed on Xian, making her feel as if they had x-ray capabilities, scanning to her core. He and Michael spoke to each other but she wasn't able to make out the language. Maybe the man didn't speak English well, but try as she might she couldn't make it out. Just what was Michael's limit she wondered? Her eyes took in the stores interior again in more detail. Over to the right near some articles hanging from the wall, she noticed what looked like the grip from a sword, only the crossguard and blade were missing. Her observation was not unnoticed by the others. As she moved closer, leaning over the counter she began to ask if she could see it.

Michael and the shopkeeper walked to where she stood. Once handed the grip, each one keenly watched her interactions with it as she ran her fingers over the surface. Slowly the memories came back to her of all the dreams and visions she'd tried to suppress since childhood. How they had always guided her decisions, warned of people and events, assured her of promises yet to come; how could she have any doubt now it was all meant to be? That she wasn't meant to be just the way she was?

With each increasing level of acceptance and faith, red-orange flickers began to appear out of the grip. They slowly formed what resembled a blade.

"What's happening?"

"Just keep holding it and believe Xian," Michael said as he leaned toward her.

The shape began to become more defined with each minute. Then the color began to change from red-orange to a bright white glow. Xian's eyes opened wider with each change of events unfolding before her. Trying to find her voice, she managed to stutter,

"Whoa…..what is this thing?"

"It is your weapon. The only tangible one you will need to fight the battles ahead," said Michael, now standing beside her.

"Xian, this is Marcus the shop keeper but really he's a guardian of many sacred items and secrets. Marcus, this is Xian, the Sword of Vengeance."

"It's great to finally meet you Xian," said Marcus smiling, "I have waited for quite some time to give you this sword."

As she smiled and slightly bowed in Marcus' direction, Michael explained that no one enters this store without Marcus' approval and most certainly they don't leave with any of its contents unless ordained to do so. With questioning eyes, she looked at Michael, who continued by telling her that there were many like him on Earth. Each of them assigned with a purpose to fulfill, since there are many battles to fight during this age.

"What you are holding is only a sword's grip. The blade however, becomes tangible only by your faith. The stronger it is, the more powerful the blade becomes. This is your first lesson," said Michael as he guided her hand to cut through a nearby metal lamp stand.

Xian watched in awe as the object fell apart. Though she'd struggled slightly while cutting it, Michael assured her that soon there would be no resistance against her strikes.

"How do I shut it off? I can't walk around with a glowing sword."

"Stop communicating with it," said Marcus who had walked to where she now stood.

"Your thoughts and desires connect with it. Just tell it to stop showing the blade and it becomes just a grip again."

Seeing the confused look on her face, Marcus grabbed a writing pad and pen. He began to draw a stick person holding a sword. While pointing at the image he said,

"This is you holding the sword when you're in need of it, say during a battle or just to practice and hone your skills. The blade feeds off your level of faith; that the power in you is greater than anything you face. As your faith level increases, so does the ability of the blade to destroy the opposition."

Marcus paused looking up at her to make sure she was taking it all in.

"Understand so far?"

"Yes."

"Now when you don't need the blade, the energy that is connected to your faith decreases. Therefore the blade dematerializes."

"But where does the blade really come from?"

Marcus looked at Michael with a raised eyebrow. Taking the cue, Michael guided Xian near the back of the store where a thin piece of fabric draped a doorway. Positioning her in front of the door, he went and stood on the other side.

"I will explain to you the reality that you now live in Xian. No longer are your eyes closed to the truth. No longer can you pretend that there isn't more to life than what you were willing to accept. There exists a spiritual world parallel to this physical one. Just like the sunglasses incident you had at the coffee shop, think of this fabric as a veil that separates the two. When we pray and believe in God to hear and give us what we've prayed for, it is created in the spiritual world first.

It is a person's level of faith that brings it into the physical one. It's just like when your blade's pulled into this realm from the spiritual one when you need it. Remember, very few really get this understanding and even less actual know how to operate in both realms." Michael observed her through the sheer fabric, glad to see she was calmer than he'd expected.

"Remember that those behind the veil can now see you and you them. This means you must know how to defend yourself and the people around you. The enemy and his minions will be coming for you to try and stop the plan of God for your life. However, I am here to see you fulfill it."

With that, Michael pushed the fabric aside and stood in front of her. Slowly she lifted her gaze and with a new sparkle of determination in her eyes she firmly said,

"Then let's get started on my training. I'm done running and hiding from a life that's shadowed me all these years. I'm sick of feeling scared, weak and helpless."

CHAPTER 4

The numbers kept coming in. As Satan expected, certain areas yielded more than others. Still he felt there should be more, especially since the world had opened up blindly to his desires, taking ideals that seemed innocent and harmless onto itself which then became the tokens of its downward spiral. He knew that his generals were still competing amongst themselves for his favor. Smiling he thought how amusing it all was; none realized he had only his future in mind. The future they thought would be theirs was not even close to the reality that awaited all who followed him on that rebellious day in Heaven. With a deep sigh he looked over the horizon. Another day was dawning and the orange-red sky reminded him yet again of the burning destiny that he'd someday face. All this time, he still held onto the slightest hope that maybe he could escape it. His real purpose for collecting so many of these lost people souls was for an exchange with God. They were His weakness. Certainly He would pardon him and grant eternity in Heaven instead of Hell just to have their souls? Still a nagging feeling deep in his heart kept tearing away at this dream.

He felt suddenly that he wasn't alone. Turning his head slightly to the right, he saw his six generals with heads bowed, standing in a straight line waiting to be acknowledged. With a deep breath, he cleared his mind and heart of the nagging doubt he'd escape his most certain end. Facing them with shoulders squared he said,

"I know you still are not sure what role Xian will play in our future, but let me just say, none of you need to worry about her."

Noticing that they still showed no reassurance on their faces, he continued,

"Today I have looked at the numbers and noticed that there is a surge of followers in the city she lives in. Go to Miami and work on these people who will assist us in owning that city."

With his finger, Satan wrote in the air the names of three people which appeared as bright red letters. After a few moments they began to fade then disappeared. Each general mentally noted them and looked at Satan awaiting further instructions.

Without looking at either of them, Satan said,

"Each of you has a stronghold. Continue to gather souls and push these three completely on our side. Beelzebub, turn their pride up and fill them with self-serving ambitions. Carreau, get inside their hearts and harden them towards all truth. I don't want anyone telling them things to make us look bad. I want them to be deaf to all other voices. Dagon, you already have many following you with symbols they don't even understand are yours. Use their subconscious to help shape actions which will give me total control over their minds. Verrine whenever you see they are slow to act, fill them with impatience and motivate them into action."

Satan paused for a moment now looking past them all at nothing in particular. He was searching for the words to appease the last two members of his inner circle. Understanding that he had to show no favoritism he slowly said while looking directly at Azazel and Meresin,

"For you two, I have plans that will need your special abilities later in this game. Just be prepared to help deal with the influx of souls these three monkeys, whose names I gave, will direct our way."

In unison, Azazel and Meresin shouted yes. The others remained quiet. Before Satan could speak again, there was a bright flash of light and circling them was a small host of angles. From the midst stepped one who came close to Satan and said,

"I have come to warn you not to unleash your plans on these people. If you take no further action, we will leave. If you decide not to heed this warning, be prepared to fight and loose more of your minions in the process."

With a sudden roar of laughter, Satan turned around to face his generals, all of whom were wearily eyeing the host that surrounded them.

"You should be bowing before me, begging for your life. How dare you command me?"

Slowly he turned to face the angel, walking closer until he stopped within inches of him. With as calm a voice as he could muster, Satan hissed,

"Tell Him I will not change my plans nor will I be threatened to do so. This is my world and I decide what happens here. Now take your foot soldiers and leave me before I send you back alone, half tore to shreds crawling to His feet."

With that the angel and host vanished. A little surprised at how quickly the situation was settled, Satan regained his composure and turned to his generals getting ready to dismiss them.

"My lord, there is trouble in the Northern territories. We are under attack by a host of angels. Many have already been killed and we are greatly outnumbered at this time since half our force was dispatched to the East," said a lower ranking demon cowering behind the row of generals before Satan.

"What do you want us to do?" asked Meresin who was eager to take on a good fight. It had been quite some time since he battled any worthy opponents.

With clenched fist Satan slowly said to him,

"Go and create a powerful lightning storm. Kill as many as you can until reinforcements can get there."

Looking now at Azazel, he ordered,

"Take your minions and help distract them. They should be able to help weaken many until the other Fallen Ones arrive."

Nodding in agreement, Meresin and Azazel then left to do as they were told. With his eyes becoming red as flames, Satan cheerfully said to the ones remaining,

"Now let's have some fun. Each of you knows what to do with these three monkeys. You can find them at these places."

As he said the last sentence, Satan sent images to their minds showing the locations their targets most frequently visited. There was a church, lounge bar, and the front of two homes. One was a fairly large property while the other was a very modest one, both were in affluent neighborhoods. With that, they left Satan alone.

Standing with his hands holding his head, Satan opened his mouth and let out a long deep breath. His mind raced to try and figure out just what God was up to. Why would he send such a small number of angels to warn him made no sense at all Though there were many of them, they still weren't enough to completely destroy his hold on the Earth. He had a third of Heavens Fallen Angels under his command with countless humans turned minions. His time certainly hadn't come and his destruction was most definitely not going to be at the hand of that puppet Xian. Deciding to focus on events he could make sense of, Satan walked along the skies and continued to forge his plan of destroying Xian.

"If this little girl thinks she will put a dent in my armor, she is more delusional than any of the rest of her kind. I will make her an example for all to see. Piece by piece her remains will be laid before God and his precious Michael; I will take his confidence then his life. My tolerance for Michael's interference has come to a head; enough! He stood against me that day in Heaven and soon I will see him beg me to spare his life," mumbled Satan as he walked along.

The balance sheet was not showing the numbers much of the board expected, being that the church was the largest in the city. Bishop Thomas Strickman scratched his head trying to come up with a plan to get more money in the coffers. The debt was stacking up which meant he would soon have to downsize his way of life. No more luxury items, royal treatment vacations, custom tailoring, all paid on the church's credit card.

"Ah," he said while leaning back in his office desk chair.

Searching his mind he remembered a couple who had approached him after Sunday morning service. They were fairly new to the area and had big connections out of state.

"I know I have their business card here somewhere," he mumbled shuffling papers on his desk.

"Bingo," he said holding up the card while reaching for his desk phone to call the number listed.

With his hand about to press the last digit, he hung up the phone. Twisting his mouth, he contemplated just how far he was willing to go with outside partnerships. He had built his church from a small corner storefront to a two-story building that took up over twenty thousand square feet. As he continued to weigh his options, his cell phone vibrated in his pocket. Looking at the screen he recognized the number, though it wasn't saved in his contacts.

"Hello," he said in as calm a voice as he could manage.

"Why haven't you called me yet for the day?" the voice shrilled in his ear.

With a deep exhale Thomas replied,

"I've been extremely busy. There's a lot going on and I need to focus on putting out fires."

"Well I have a fire for you to put out. When are you coming to see me? I want to go shopping and check out that new resort in Palm Beach."

"I just can't right now, sorry. Look, I don't see how this is going to work and I really need to put an end to this…" he started but was cut off before being able to finish.

A deep voice said slowly and calmly to him from the phone,

"Listen, you poor excuse of a man. I say when this is over. Do you want your congregation to know about us? How you love the feel of another man? Now get your sorry butt over here and take me shopping."

Before Thomas could say another word, there was a click in his ear. Looking at his cell phone in fear, he threw back his head and exhaled long and loud. He began to shake his head, knowing he was in a big mess. He wondered how he had gotten into such a fix and just how he was going to get out of it. No one could ever know his secret. Thomas knew the leech that just made threats was not even worth all the attention he wasted on him. Nolan was a money hungry, life sucking opportunist. Though soon after getting close to him, Thomas understood it would mean trouble, yet Nolan's initial charms had him spellbound. Grabbing his desk phone again, he dialed the number from the business card still in his hand. On the second ring a female voice said,

"Hello, Leanne speaking."

"Oh hello Leanne, this is Bishop Strickman calling. How are you today?"

"Bishop Strickman," said Leanne as she motioned to her husband sitting across the room from her, "I'm blessed. So glad you called."

"Ah yes. I was thinking more about our conversation and wondered if you, your husband and I could meet to discuss your ideas further?"

"Of course Bishop," said Leanne as she scribbled a note about a meeting to her husband who now sat next to her, "how about this Wednesday say around 2:00pm at your office?"

"Wednesday around 2:00pm you say, let me check my calendar. Just a moment please," Thomas scrolled his calendar on his phone, "yes that would be a great time for me to meet with you both, however let's meet at the Broadwalk Restaurant & Grille on Hollywood Beach."

With a devilish smile Leanne agreed and after saying her goodbyes, looked at her husband and gushed,

"We almost have him hook, line and sinker sweat-heart. He sounded strained on the phone. This should be an easy sell."

Jeremy Mitchell clapped his hands in relief then hugged his wife. As he held her he cooed,

"See honey, I told you he was hurting. I could tell from the size of his organization and the word on the streets about his spending habits. The man is ripe for the picking. We hit a gold mine this time."

Pushing him back, Leanne looked in his eyes with a half-smile. Seeing she still had signs of worry on her

face, Jeremy kissed her then softly said,

"This will not be Chicago all over again. This time we know what not to do, so trust me and relax. Soon we will be rolling in money again and all those that turned their backs on us will come crawling to be in our circle."

Jeremy stood up and walked over to the living room window. He stared out over the city's skyline in the distance remembering the tall luxury penthouses he drove by whenever he felt down. Soon they would be back in the life and own one of those units. He smiled and turned to face Leanne, who was quietly watching him from the sofa, and said,

"Trust me, all those who kicked us when things went bad, they'll surely pay to get back in our world. That beautiful city out there in the distance will be our future stomping ground. We're going to own a piece of Miami and live it up with the rest of the elite."

Turning back to stare out the window, Jeremy smiled as he planned not to have them dipping into their savings for much longer. Besides something had to break as the money was getting low faster than he had calculated. Miami was not cheap and putting on a good front cut their survival budget almost in half. They needed money fast and whatever it took to make this deal work, Jeremy was all in.

Leanne could tell from Jeremy's body language he was formulating his plan. She had long learned to never underestimate him. He was sweet but could be calculating and cruel when things didn't go his way. She knew of the secret journal he kept in the back of his sock drawer. Pages full of all the people who did him wrong with side notes of the revenge he planned to take on each of them. Though she loved him, she never thought of leaving because his journal was not where she wanted her name to ever be listed. Shaking the thoughts from her head, she looked at him and slowly smiled. Of all the girls he could have chosen, she was the one who landed the most coveted role on their college campus. Paired in her first few months of attending, she never gave another man a second glance.

She knew the hateful stares girls gave her and the wanting looks they gave Jeremy. None of that matters now. For three years they've been husband and wife. Three years of living in the fast lane. Chicago was just a taste of the good life they both promised each other they'd share. Miami was going to be the place that they perfected their skills to reach goals planned. Miami was the place they would finally show the world, they had arrived.

Michael and Xian sat on a park bench not far from Marcus' store. People hurried by focused on their destinations, consumed with their lives. As she watched them pass, Xian's eyes began to lose focus while her mind reflected on wondering how many of them really knew what was going on. After observing her for a while from the corner of his eye, Michael said softly,

"In order to know how to defeat your opponent, you need to know where they come from; whom and what they hold most dear."

His voice brought her back to the moment from her wondering thoughts. She slightly turned to face him and listened intently until she only heard his voice. Seeing he had her undivided attention,

"Not sure just what you know about Satan, but I will go over his existence just the same. I need you understand how he thinks and his motives. He was first called Lucifer, referred to as Day Star or Son of the Morning, a once highly exalted angel. God created him to be a minister of heavenly worship, music; his body was covered in precious stones and he was what you would consider breathtaking to look at. Lucifer was not just an angel, but a covering one. Similar as to the cherubim whose job it was to cover the mercy seat of the Ark of the Covenant, God created him to forever be in heaven's throne room; in God's very presence."

"You mean he actual was before God all the time?" asked Xian, eyes losing focus again as she mindlessly stared.

"Yes, Lucifer was perfect; nothing was plain or ordinary about him. He was a true representation of his name Son of the Morning."

Taking hold of her shoulders until he saw her focusing again on him, Michael continued,

"He was filled with wisdom at a level far greater that other angels. You could say Lucifer understood the ways of God well. He is not a fool Xian; he is cunning and skilled at his abilities. But even he is no match for the Creator."

After pausing for a few seconds, making sure his words registered in her mind Michael said,

"However, for all that he was, he is now only a fraction of it. Now he is a Fallen One, better known as Satan, stripped of his heavenly position and privileges in heaven but not his beauty. This he uses most to have his way."

With a sigh Michael bowed his head slightly. His eyes seemed to be focused on some distant memory replaying itself. Slowly Xian touched his right arm to bring him back. He began to speak again as he raised his head until their eyes locked.

"On the day Lucifer decided he would be like God, he had managed to persuade one-third of the angels in heaven to follow him. He promised them a new order which would grant them freedom from servitude to God. So began the war between Satan and his third of heaven's angels against the rest of us. It was like nothing any of us had ever seen."

"Why didn't God just destroy Satan and stop the war? Wouldn't that have been easier?" asked Xian in an exasperated tone.

Michael stared at her with a blank expression. He thought how all humans wanted the easy way out. Instant results and gratification; such spoiled things there are.

"God is merciful Xian and even when Satan dared to become full of pride, he still showed mercy. Isn't that what you constantly ask for in your heart from God; mercy?"

Signing and nodding her head, Xian began to blush from embarrassment. She certainly cried out for Gods mercy on a regular basis. How grateful she was to him that despite all she does, he still grants it to her.

"Besides, God's plan for mankind included Satan and his fallen angles. Through them mankind would be tested and their faith tried. They would become like the replacement of the third lost to Satan's ambitions. Mankind would be the occupants of the new kingdom God would give his beloved son, Jesus Christ."

As if a light went off in Xian's head, a twinkle showed in her eyes. Seeing she finally understood the reason for the fight she's been made a part of, Michael stood up and reached for her hand. Once she was standing, he told her to trust him and not be afraid. Before she could show or verbalize agreement, they were high above the earth in the clouds looking down. Knowing she would panic, Michael pulled her to him and held her still. With eyes wide open and speechless, Xian stared at the Earth. It was so beautiful from high up. Slowly she could see shapes forming in the sky, they moved in random patterns. Understanding her finger pointing gesture Michael explained,

"Those are some of The Fallen. The ones who have no human body to possess, yet even in their current state, they still torment people."

"Why did you bring me here?"

"So you can get a small view of how God sees His creation in all of its beauty, despite how Satan tries to corrupt it. This is what you are fighting for. All of those souls down there who still live clueless lives and those that have hardened their hearts towards Gods truth; you fight because He is merciful towards them."

Tears began to fill her eyes as she reflected on all the times people came to her rescue when she felt like she would lose her mind and life. For all those God had used to show her mercy. Seeing the world from high above and thinking on the multitude of lost souls she took a deep breath and whispered,

"Forgive me Heavenly Father for being such a coward and ungrateful. Help me to be strong and do your will."

Looking up at Michael she smiled,

"I will do whatever you ask. Whenever I feel unable to carry on, please remind me of this moment."

With a smile he nodded and as quickly as they got up into the sky, they returned back to Earth.

CHAPTER 5

Carreau stood watching Thomas as he squirmed in his office chair. Happy to see that he was becoming more and more deaf to the sound of God's voice with each passing day; deeper he fell into the bondage of homosexuality. Eyes shrouded with his fleshly desires, he no longer looked at the women parading themselves before him. Had he known his actions would open the gates to allow other perversions to invade his church, Carreau wondered if Thomas would have fasted and prayed the way he should have in order to help those being drawn to this church building. Carreau had surveyed the place and saw less and less residue of holiness there. Symbols of Dagon-worshipping and rituals had also taken root in the place. Eagerness to be like the famous ones on television, Thomas had aligned himself with any that would let him even peek into their world. Carreau and his demon foot soldiers were making good headway on turning the minds and hearts of the congregation.

The rippling effects of Thomas' choices were following each of the new members home, setting up roots there to consume entire families; binding generations to come. Carreau laughed now, knowing that he couldn't be heard. How easy this assignment was going to be. His personal reaping through this church alone was going to make him shine before Satan. *Whatever it takes to stay on his good side, I'm game.* Rubbing his hands together, Carreau orchestrated a plan to help solidify his hold on Thomas. Grinning and staring intently at Thomas' frame while he walked out his office, Carreau remembered Jeremy and Leanne Mitchell. He figured they would be perfect pawns for his scheme, serving as a means to even infiltrate circles of those outside this church.

All Richard wanted was to give into the exhaustion that now claimed his body. He was even too tired to smile when seeing his bed. Somehow he managed to shower and half dress himself before falling onto the firm mattress. Thoughts swirled in his head as if in a mixing bowl. With eyelids no longer obeying the mental signals to stay open, now tightly shut, Richard did his best to clear his mind and focus on the growing black dot at the center of the spinning images. The larger it grew, the deeper in sleep he fell until he was knocked out. He hoped Satan was too busy with other matters to pay him any attention tonight. Unknowingly, Richard was in for a good night's sleep. His body surely needed it. Life for him was going to get more strenuous with an internal war about to begin.

As he floated in the darkness of his dream, a dim memory surfaced of his grandfather. He and Richard were fishing near a lake. It was one of the few peaceful times in his childhood. His grandfather was gentle with him just as his mother always was. Trying to focus on the words he was saying, Richard strained his ears to hear. The older man was pointing at the lake saying,

"See son how calm the water looks on the surface? Underneath though is a busy world of fish. This is how people can appear to us sometimes; calm on the outside but busy like a strong wind deep inside," picking Richard up he continued, "remember son, whenever you feel like a strong wind is blowing you all around on the inside, pray. Prayer will give you the strength to destroy your fears. Prayer will make you strong and God will fight your enemies for you."

Then slowly the image faded and darkness surrounded him again. His mother's smiling face appeared next in front of him. She had no bruises on her face from his father's fists, no tears in her bloodshot eyes; just a sweet big smile. Reaching out to touch her cheek, his hand just wasn't long enough to reach it. Each step he took towards her still didn't get him close enough. Soon he was running, trying to reach where she was, but the distance never shortened. Dropping to his knees he began to cry, covering his face with his hands as he did.

"Just believe in me," a voice spoke. It was calm and had an authoritative tone, "just believe in me and I will give you peace."

Richard looked around trying to find the source of the voice. It wasn't Buddy, he was certain of that. This voice was different. This one caressed his ears like the softness of his blanket. Could the voice be that of God he wondered. *Why would God speak to me now after all this time?* He was so tied up with bad thoughts and Buddy said he was the only friend he really had or needed. *Yet grandfather said God would make me stronger and I Richard feel very weak at this point.* Being weak and mentally drained had become his reality. The thought of peace was too fleeting a wish to even consider.

Slowly Richard's eyes opened. He had slept soundly through the night for the first time in as long as he could remember. His body was rested, a feeling he almost had forgotten. A smile was on his face when he rubbed the remaining sleep from his eyes. Amazed he reflected on his dreams. Warm loving feelings washed over him as he replayed the images of his grandfather and mother. The last message now echoed in his ears. Repeating the words out loud as he walked to his bathroom, he looked beyond his reflection in the mirror. He said them several times as if doing so was the only way to make the loving sensation stay with him.

Mindlessly he dressed for work and due to a detour, took a side street which that parked him in front of a little church as he waited for the red light to turn green. The stain glass windows sparkled in the morning sun. Without even knowing why, Richard turned into its parking lot and approached the front door. As soon as his hand reached for the doorknob, Buddy's voice asked,

"What are you doing so early this morning Richard? Am I not always available to talk to? No one in there will really understand your pain like I do. Come now, turn around and head to work. You don't want to be late."

Standing frozen starting to feel defeated, Richard looked at the doorknob only inches away from his hand. He felt if he could just touch it, some power would fill him providing the strength to finally get away from Buddy.

"Move it!" Buddy's voice now shouted.

With his head bowed, Richard turned and walked back to his car and drove away; overcome with regret. Buddy was mumbling something about their unbreakable bond and reminding him of all the times he was there when Richard needed comforting. All his efforts to drown him out were futile, so he drove in almost autopilot mode to work. Deep in his heart he felt a dull pain; he hated what he had become and desperately wanted a way to change. Exhaling slowly he placed the car ignition into park and turned it off. Slamming the door, he pretended it was Buddy's face the rolled up window was smashing into. Satan could see from Richard's eyes that something was trying to work against him. No way was this little puppet cutting the strings. Too much time and effort were invested in this one. Whether he liked it or not, he was going to play his part out until the end; or wish he had, Satan swore.

CHAPTER 6

It felt as if Xian always had Michael around. She doubted she could go a day without him near; her strength feeds off of his. As promised, she trained daily under his direction. Her body though fit, in the beginning felt out of shape and strained against the vigorous workouts he put her through. Michael's strategy was to not only build her stamina, but make her more agile. Her muscles had become quite stretched and she even surprised herself at times of just how flexible she'd become. They trained early each morning before she went to work, listening as Michael explained tactics she had to know when fighting spiritual beings. Xian was a sponge. He was pleased to see how she retained all he said, never doubting his faith in her.

While eating dinner at a small American diner, a place they visited at least once a week to get some people watching don, Xian demonstrated how good she'd become at spotting shadows that outlined people who were under Satan's control. The first time she scoped out the restaurant, Michael had to grab her hand to help control the panic which tried to take over her mind. She had to stare at her water glass for a good five minutes to get control of her emotions as the drained blood slowly came back into her face.

"You will learn to not be surprised by what you see after a while. I know it's a shock, but you're safe. Shadows are like residue from when the demons last used a person's body. Those that are currently being used, you will see the demon itself inside. And yes, they can see you looking at them."

Once she had calmed down he continued,

"They will not approach you unless ordered to do so by their direct commander; one of Satan's five generals. Most of the time, they'll just watch and observe your actions; reporting information back to their commander who will then decide what action to take. Trust me; they know you're capable of destroying them, even with the little training you've gotten so far."

It was then that he decided she was ready for her first fight; that was just three nights ago. Now they were traveling out of the city, Xian hadn't asked where and Michael didn't offer any information about where they were headed. After about forty minutes, they were parked in front of what appeared to be a pretty expensive gated community. Xian looked at the row of houses as the car made its way through the winding streets. There were only a few people outside, either walking to their cars or tending to immaculate lawns. Michael could sense her guard was down; the seemingly peaceful neighborhood had put her at ease. His face suddenly showed a scowling expression. He soon would correct this; she needs to be always alert and ready to strike.

Michael parked near a side entrance to a large building near a gated pool and playground. Xian guessed it to be the community center and leisurely strolled along following him through the door. The sounds of classical music greeted them and as they rounded a corner, several people were exercising over at the far end of the room. There were others sitting and chatting near the center in oversized stuffed chairs. All seemed nice and peaceful.

"This is a nice change of scenery," Xian said as she turned around taking in the space, "are we here to meet someone?"

"Yes we are in a way. Tell me, how does this place make you feel?" Michael asked, now intently looking at her while she continued to casually look around the room.

"It makes me feel carefree," Xian replied as she turned to face him, "but appearances can fool you," she said now with a face void of the clueless expression she had a moment ago.

Michael saw she was learning to mask her emotions pretty good. She even had him fooled. With a growing grin and snap of his fingers, Xian saw one of the people who were chatting in the center of the room, now to Michaels back, jump in the air and lunge towards her. It was a woman holding a long staff, where it came from Xian wasn't sure but her instincts told her to side step and aim low at her attacker's body. The fiery blade of Xian's sword was struck by an end of the staff as its wielder landed a few feet from her. As if someone else was moving her body like a puppet master, Xian felt herself twist and bend, striking and blocking the movements of the woman. What snapped her from the daze was when her body ran up a side wall now near her twisting mid-air, landing behind the woman; sword at the base of her skull.

"Stop," Michael bellowed from behind her.

Xian stayed frozen but didn't break her stance. Realizing she wouldn't until unarmed, the woman dropped her staff and held up her arms. Only then did Xian back away, eyes still fixed on the woman as she backed up to stand near Michael. Without looking at her he said,

"Nice moves. You handled that well but that was just one attacker. They won't be fair and fight you one at a time," Michael said as moving in a flash to the opposite side of the room, leaving Xian alone now encircled by five people, some with weapons, others bare handed.

"Don't worry about hurting any of them; they'll heal after a while. Just don't follow through on any kill moves, got it?"

"Got it," Xian huffed as she slowly turned facing each person, looking for the slightest sign as to who was

going to attack first.

She felt the sudden displacement of air behind her right side. Slightly turning her body to create less of a target she saw a man unarmed reaching out to grab her. Tripping him she struck hard with the pommel of her sword in the center of his back before he lay sprawled across the floor groaning. As he was falling two others had started to attack from either side of her. Grabbing the one closest to her around the neck, Xian used her momentum to bring them down while landing a hard roundhouse kick square on the side of the other attackers head. With only a few seconds to reinforce her balance, she crouched low, getting ready for the last two who now headed her way in single file. With strikes to the legs, blocking another sword then a chain, she moved between them standing in the spot they had advanced from. Instead of waiting for them to make a move, she ran for the one to her right, climbing them like the wall moments ago, striking them in the stomach, chest then forehead and she propelled upwards and towards the other aiming for their heart.

"Kill move!" She heard Michael warn.

With just seconds before her blade would claim its target, she threw her sword to her left hand, hitting the spot above the attacker's heart with her fist instead. Landing with a rollout she slowly stood, senses high anticipating more attacks from the ones looking on standing near Michael.

"Not bad. You used the wall and their bodies well to assist you in your attacks. Still need to work on your speed a bit, but for the most part your close quarter's skills are pretty impressive. However, they aren't what you will really be fighting. Your enemy will attack however they can so you need to learn how to use your most powerful weapon," Michael said.

Looking at her sword, she asked,

"Isn't this my most powerful weapon?"

With a smile Michael walked up to her placing his finger inches away from her chest then said,

"In here lives your most powerful weapon. The day you learn to truly release from here, will be the day the fight's certainly going to come to you. Come have a seat, I want you to meet some folks."

Michael introduces the group of people to Xian. He explains that all who live in the community are actually angels. It is one of the several places in the State where other humans are trained to fight and use their gifts. Seeing the question in her eyes before she could speak it he confirmed she would have found her way here long ago if she hadn't denied her gift the opportunity to develop when she was younger; they would have met under different circumstances.

There were a few more skill tests, each one a little harder than the one before. Xian noticed that the speed of the attacks increased each round and wondered if she was really as good as Michael claimed she was. He could see the doubt creeping in her eyes just a little during the last match. Just as she thought it was over, Michael stepped in and went to work on the last two opponents. Their movements increased to a blur before Xian and she thought for sure there was no way she would ever move that fast.

As the fight continued, she said a little prayer in her heart, asking God to help her further develop the skills to fight spiritual enemies. For a moment she closed her eyes while praying and saw Michael and the others clearly. They were moving at what she considered a relatively normal speed. She could see the strikes and blocks; hear the grunts and groaning sounds they each made. Opening her eyes she looked again, only to see their movements as before in a blur. With closed eyes again she looked and realized this was yet another skill she had learned; to see without using her natural eyes, but to rely on using spiritual means to see spiritual things.

The fighting stopped and now they were all looking at her. With eyes still closed, she saw their true forms. They still had the form of a man but light emanated from them, some brighter than others; some more white, some more gold. She looked into Michaels' eyes, only this time they were opposite that of his brown pools. The eyes she looked at were silver irises with specs of white, the center of which were an electric light blue.

"I can see you," she whispered as he walked closer, "I mean really see you. I can see all of you."

"Yes Xian, this is what we really look like. You have tapped into another gift. It will help you better at finding the enemy when you need to. With this gift you can see who is possessed. You'll also be faster when you fight if you don't use your natural eyes in the beginning," Michael said taking her hand, placing it on her chest,

"Do you see that spark of light inside you?"

Xian moved her hand then nodded, exposing more of what looked like a spark of white light, flickering inside her.

"For you to become most powerful, you need to learn to let it grow. Your level of faith in God will determine how much light is at work inside you. It was your little prayer in faith to God to help you be stronger that allowed you to see in the spiritual world; to see us fight and as we really are. Now imagine if you had more faith in Him to fill you with His power?" Michael said, pausing to let the words register in her whirling mind.

Holding out his hand, he pointed to a table near the front door. On it was a vase filled with flowers. Instructing Xian to close her eyes, he then released a tiny ball of light from his hand. The light hit one of the flower buds in the vase, slicing it clean from its stem, rolling off the table onto the floor. He motioned for her to go and inspect it closer. As Xian stooped to pick up the bud, she looked at the vase of flowers. None of the others were damaged and the stem had a clean cut where the bud once was. With eyes wide she looked back at Michael,

"Are you trying to say I can do this? I mean I can shoot balls of light from my hands also?"

"Once you learn to tap into your gift and control your human nature, you'll be able to do so much more,"

Michael said as he crossed the space between them. "You have learned quite a bit in a short period, but you are no match for any of Satan's generals, let alone Satan himself. We still have much training to do," taking the bud from her hand placing it back on its stem. When he moved his hand away, Xian laughed when she saw the flower was intact, without any sign of the previous mutilation.

"You got to be kidding me. Seriously, I'll be able to do that too?" she said almost snorting as she did.

Michael continued walking towards the side door they originally entered through, pausing long enough to turn and look her square in the face and said,

"Only if you have the faith strong enough to believe, Xian; faith is the key haven't you realized this yet?"

Before she could reply he had turned and walked out the door. Feeling like she was just slapped in the face, Xian turned red with shame. Of course she understood how important faith was, but being checked on it stung, not to mention how embarrassed she felt in front of the others, supposedly being the Sword of Revenge and all.

The ride back to the city was long and quiet. As the sun began to set Xian's body started shutting down. Muscles were stiffening; stomach beginning to growl. All the hand to hand tests and training had used up more energy than she could have imagined. The only things she wanted now were a hot plate of food and an even hotter shower. Images of her bed with the city skyline as a backdrop flooded her mind. She couldn't remember when she wanted to just fall onto it more than at that moment. The car turned in the opposite direction of her apartment and with that, she pushed up in the seat. Looking over at Michael, she could see from his expression, he was planning something; hoping it included some food turning her gazed to the oncoming scenery. She hadn't been on this side of town before. *It's amazing how you can live so much of your life within just a few miles radius of home and work.* Almost lost she tried to look at the tops of the tall buildings to get an idea of where they were.

Soon as she thought she'd made out the name on a few building tops, Michael swerved off the main road. The sound of crunching gravel covering a parking lot between two buildings was all she now heard. The one on her left was that of a multi-office complex. Dim lights lined the outside lobby area, and along the side corridors of the building, casting eerie shadows along the low lined hedges. The other looked deserted except for the light on the top floor, smiling and shaking her head slightly she followed Michael towards it, thinking how of course this was the one he'd be taking her to.

Aching muscles were all but forgotten, the adrenaline starting to make its way through her again. She tried to step quietly as possible, but the gravel stones continued to grind against each other under her feet. Seeing it was a hopeless battle, Michael grabbed her by the waist, gave her that hold on stare and before she could complete blinking, they were on the rooftop.

"This is not a drill Xian. Inside on the top floor there is a group of possessed that have been slowly taking this area block by block. The floors below, except the main one, are full of demons waiting for bodies to claim. So, no holding back on the kill moves and this is no time to lose faith either. Don't worry; your sword won't harm the human bodies, only the dark spirits possessing them. Once free, the people will appear dazed but they'll be fine. My brothers will guide them home and help their minds adjust to what has happened to them."

"What do you mean your brothers?" Xian asked

a little confused, "ah you mean other angles, okay, got it."

"Remember the flower and trust your senses. Don't believe all your natural eyes tell you. Behind the innocent smiles is a destructive demon who would be more than happy to be the one to kill you for Satan," Michael said as he descended the staircase, stopping at the landing just outside the top floors exit door.

With a deep long cleansing breath, Xian calmed her mind and emotions. She focused her thoughts on what was beyond the door. Drew from the knowledge of past events and slowly felt the flicker in her chest grow into a constant flame. By the time Michael opened the door and the possessed headed towards them, Xian was thirty percent charged and with eyes closed she saw them for what they were. This helped her not focus on the human bodies they were using; made her surer with each swing of her sword and movement of her body. All of her fears turned into fuel that made her faith stronger. Everything she knew to be true and those she knew to be lies propelled her forward.

Michael worked with little effort to clear a good amount of them. As he did, he watched smiling as Xian moved faster and faster. If she could see herself, she probably would be in awe of the sight. The remaining crowd was now coming at her in an almost constant stream. Like a tree trimmer, she laid them to waste one by one. It was a beautiful site to Michael's eyes. With the last one falling to the floor, Xian spun around, looking to see if there were any left that want to challenge her. The rush of energy coursed through her; the sword she held blade was burning a deep orange. Each time she used it now, Michael noticed the shade got lighter.

Walking to her he said in a calm voice,

"There aren't any more here tonight. How do you feel?"

"I feel like electricity and fire are all over me. I feel like I could burst out of my skin," she said staring at the flaming sword in her hand then up into his eyes.

"Good. Soon you will be able to feel it less and guide the flow of the energy from your body outward. Remember the flower today? That is how I did it. I controlled the flow and focused it on the flower," Michael said to her, lowering her hand with the sword so she would start to gain control of herself

"Take long deep breaths, nice and slow. That's it. Continue until you have calmed your emotions," he said as they walked back towards the roof top.

"How did I do?" Xian asked when they stood under the night sky.

"You did great. Did time slow down for you as you fought?" Michael asked, knowing it did.

"Yes, it was as if I was moving in slow motion, the way you did when you were fighting earlier. Does that mean I was moving as fast as you did?" Xian asked, excitement now filling her eyes. With a small chuckle, Michael nodded then said,

"You looked like a gardener chopping away at a hedge. It was beautiful."

The piercing sounds of screams vibrated through the walls of the buildings lower levels. Bodiless the demons swirled around frantically, not sure if to leave or stay. *Would they be next to face the Sword of Revenge?* Just before the last shrill cry, Carreau appeared on the level just below where Xian stood. He assured the restless group that they were safe and how Xian was only on a training run. He had been watching her and Michael all day and advised that her powers were still weak; she was no match for all of them. This Carreau knew was a lie but the last thing he wanted was to have a panic in his lower ranks. Besides, this supply of demons was to embody the next wave of lost people who would be blindly following Bishop Thomas Strickman.

Carreau waited until Michael and Xian left before throwing a carrot to the riled bunch around him. He decided to pacify them a little more by sharing his plans regarding Strickman's church members. This seemed to work for the moment, but Carreau knew it wouldn't keep them in check long. He really could use a break. At the pace Xian was training, he would soon lose more foot soldiers than he could afford. He weighed the odds of him taking her out. At her current skill level, he very well might be able to end this nuisance. Also, it would surely solidify his permanent place in Satan's good graces. He smiled to himself thinking how it really could work, but then the smile quickly faded when he remembered Michael demonstrating how to tap into her inner power cutting the bud off from its stem. Rubbing his neck, Carreau decided to observe for a little longer to better assess what he was going up against.

CHAPTER 7

The past few weeks were full of peaceful days, well at least to Richard they were. No voices or strange feelings of being watched. He actually was able to get through the day without having to act normal. Yet he was having all too real dreams every other night. Interestingly enough, Jenny was in most of them, though not in the way he would have wanted. There was no gradual buildup, neither was there any fade out just before he woke. Then there were the little bruises; seemingly small but Richard had no memory of how they got there.

The dreams all had a similar theme. He would be in what appeared as a ballroom with floor length deep red curtains, covering most of the walls. There was only the sound of groans and occasional cries as if the person was being forced to do something against their will. Dimmed lights from vintage chandeliers provided just enough illumination for Richard to see only about four feet in front of him clearly. No matter where he turned, he couldn't escape the smell of burning incense trying to mask the scent of charred flesh. Holding a hand over his nose and mouth he pushed his way through a thickening crowd.

A soft hand takes his other one and pulls him deeper into the room. It's Jenny leading him. Try as he may, he's unable to see where they're headed. Then he sees a table laden with branding irons. Each with brands glowing red from the heat, but there is no visible fire. He looks around for the heat source, seeing none. Jenny, now seated backward in a chair next to the table, raises her blouse just enough to expose a few inches of her lower back. The weight of one of the brands brings Richards attention to his free hand. Puzzled he stares at it for a moment, not remembering taking it from the table.

As if someone else was moving his limbs, Richard brands Jenny just to the left of the spine. She doesn't scream as he would've expected, just sits there looking away holding the hem of her shirt. Then she gets up and is immediately replaced by another person, waiting to be branded. As if he were a robot on an assembly line, Richard brands each person one after the other. This continues for a while, and then he's standing on a rooftop looking out over a burning city. There's smoke everywhere and the heat cuts his breath short. Branded people walk aimlessly along the streets below. He sees Jenny approaching him from the corner of his eye.

Turning to face her, he notices she looks different. As she gets closer, Richard sees her eyes are blood red and her skin no longer pale white, but golden brown with her once solid red hair now streaked with black. She appears to be practically gliding as she moves closer to him. When almost in front of him, hands stretched out to grab, he wakes up. Just like the mornings before, sweat covers his body, his skin warm to the touch and his throat is nearly parched. As if living in a loop, he jumps into the tub and starts a cold shower, lapping like an animal from cupped hands while standing under the flowing water.

Whatever the dream was about, Richard didn't really care. His days were free of Buddy and that was beginning to be worth the night sweats. The dream didn't frighten him. He was long desensitized by his life's events. Before he longed to find solace in sleep; now he tried his best to stay awake. Whichever state of mind Buddy was present in, Richard found himself wanting to be in the opposite. Being around Jenny tugged at the small hope of normalcy; for the first time in countless days, he really observed people around him. He noticed their carefree movements, big genuine smiles, embraces. He wondered what he'd have to do to taste just a little of that freedom.

This fool really thinks he's free of me, Satan thought to himself. Perched on a cloud he gazed down to the Earth noticing the pattern his branded ones made. From his vantage point, they formed almost the shape of a rose; crisscrossing the city landscape. Now laughing he thought of how Richard believed his dreams were just that, dreams. The lost man had no idea just how real it all was. No idea to the fact that with each brand he made on a new body, a

piece of his soul was lost with it.

Satan looked at his right hand, mimicking the movements he did while controlling Richard's hand during the branding process. It was Satan's grips that left the little bruises on Richard. Ones from forcing him to brand and the other from carrying him to the rooftop to take in the new world Satan planned to create.

"Yeah," Satan mumbled to himself, "no way this fool is breaking free; too much invested and not enough time to start over. Richard and Jenny will be my Adam and Eve."

Xian lied in bed, awake but eyes closed. Ever since meeting Michael she woke before her alarm clock chimed. Her mind playing over the prior day's events, self-evaluating her progress with regard to fighting, controlling her sword and most importantly her faith in her ability to meet up to the great expectation her life had become. Each day felt as if she'd just woken from a long dream. Yet the possibility of it all being a dream swiftly vanished whenever she picked up her sword's grip, then solidified again when she saw Michael. Dressed for work, she tried to focus on the growing pile of papers on her desk. She needed to learn to focus on what was in front of her, work was necessary to pay for living. Michael said nothing about that part of her life changing. Determined to get caught up, she hurried along, noticing the beauty of the city in the rising sunlight for a change. She looked beyond the growing crowd of commuters, trying to keep her thoughts from wondering which one she may face soon with her sword. Being next to them on the sidewalk was different than passing in her car, as today she decided to walk, getting in some exercise in the process.

  Michael had been watching her as he stood on a rooftop nearby. He was always watching over her lately, surprised that there were no attacks on her yet. Wondering what the others were waiting for, he scanned the people along the now busy street. No one in particular caught his attention. Then an unhuman like speed yanked his gaze to the left; the person darted amongst the crowds half a block behind Xian. Grinning he nodded his head,

  "I see you. Did you guys really think I wouldn't be on the lookout?" Michael said, "Just how many of you are on her trail this morning, huh?"

Seeing that Xian was almost at her office building, Michael continued to scan the area. His gaze moved from rooftops to the street, in total he counted six tracking her. The two on the rooftops he decided to leave for last. Four at street level were moving in fast. In an instant Michael was face to face with the one closest to Xian. His right hand touched the chest of the woman, displacing the demon inside her before she had a chance to block his arm. By the time she managed to realize where she was, Michael had made his way onto the next follower. He moved to fast for anyone to actually see him, most felt only a quick breeze as he went past. The second follower was a young man dressed in jeans and a t-shirt wearing headphones. His head bopped to the beats coming from them while his eyes stayed fixed on the back of Xian's head. So focused on his target, he didn't even notice Michael first yanking the headphones from his ears then standing behind him, the heat of Michael's hand pressing against his back.

With some hesitation, this demon clawed at the young man's body, not wanting to leave it. He turned his head and looked over the man's right shoulder, eyes locking with Michael's for only a brief moment, before turning away letting out a piercing scream. Michael, with his hand still on the man's back, spoke to the demon that then immediately disappeared. His scream, however, alerted the remaining four who were tracking Xian. As if with a hive mentality, they all rushed towards her. Michael seeing this, within seconds was holding Xian against him and taking her to the rooftop where one of the followers was approaching from.

Knowing she would have little time to react, he released his hold on her and stood by watching to see what she'd do next. After a few blinks of her eyes, Xian understood what was about to happen. Either she defended herself or this screaming woman was going to do some real damage. Instinctively she reached for the grip of her sword. The blade materialized as it drew strength from her faith. Closing her eyes for a brief moment she saw the demon inside the woman; it would be upon her within the next five steps. In a sprint Xian moved towards her, sword extended in her left hand. The woman leaned to Xian's right, trying to stay out of the path of the oncoming blade. When they were only one step away from each other, Xian switched the sword to her right hand. With a cut to the throat, the woman took two more steps forward then fell face first to the ground. The demon dissipated once its decapitated form left her body.

Before she had time to replay the past few moments, Michael had them both back down on the street below. They backed into an alley once making sure the remaining three followers saw them; two men and a woman each now holding something in their hands to use as weapons. Michael stood just behind Xian as they readied themselves for the oncoming attacks. Xian waited until attacked before breaking her stance. One of the men now holding what had appeared to be an umbrella, which had transformed into a steel rod, came at her swinging it wildly. Surprising even herself with the amount of agility she had, Xian twisted and turned her upper body, all the while shortening the distance between them until she had her swords blade deep into the man's heart. She didn't stop moving forward until the crossguard of her sword was flush against his chest.

Using his body as a shield Xian forced the woman, who had quickly approached from behind the man, up against the nearby building while her protruding blade anchored into her chest. Only after she saw the demons leave their bodies did she remove her blade. The remaining follower proved to be more of a challenge. He was obviously trained to fight. He landed a roundhouse kick to her shoulder, taking her down to one knee. She spotted Michael leaning up against the opposite building smiling at her. Finally getting that he was not intending to assist, she looked back at the man who was getting ready to charge again.

Deciding to take his legs out, she stayed low and swept him off balance. When he crashed hard on his back, Xian pounced over him and had her sword aimed for this chest. Using her entire body weight, she tried to hit her target but the man wasn't giving it up so easily. With a raised knee, he was able to push her off and jump back on his feet. With deep breaths, Xian looked him over. She was already late for work, not to mention her clothes were dirty and rumbled. Understanding that brute force wasn't going to do much good, she relaxed her shoulders and drew from the well of faith inside her. Calmly she opened her eyes and waited for him to attack. Despite his offense, Xian full of confidence held her sword tight and like a samurai in movies she'd seen, she firmly planted her feet. As if she was being controlled by someone else, she sidestepped and made one long cut upwards in the air. Nothing was heard but the swish of air, disturbed by her movement and followed by the faint cry of the demon as it vanished. It took her a moment to control her emotions that now wanted to consume her. Michael held her right shoulder with his hand to help her calm down.

"Breathe," he said "you did a good job."

Taking her hand now, he smiled and led her further into the alley. As they walked her clothes became clean and straightened. She didn't notice at first, her mind still racing and senses heightened from the fight. Michael waited for her to look at him before he said,

"You did it all on your own, so be kind to yourself. We still need to work on your speed though. That last kick shouldn't have landed on you. Yet overall not bad for your first real fight; we'll also work on you observation skills."

"I didn't even realize I was being followed," Xian said, "were you following me?"

"I keep an eye out for you, yes. I expected you'd have more encounters by now, but nevertheless, we'll use whoever they send for target practice. You need to get to work. I'll see you later," Michael said before disappearing near the end of the alley.

Still feeling wired, Xian walked to work. She did everything she could to appear normal once stepping into her office. The busy sounds of coworkers helped drown the demon screams in her head. Her name was already being yelled out and questions were being shot off in rapid succession. Time to shift mental gears and she actually welcomed the distractions. It would be time enough to work on speed and observation techniques. Right now she had an earthly job to attend to; deadlines to meet. If nothing else spiritual tried to interfere, she might just make her goal of clearing her desk by this evening.

"Looks like another working lunch," she mumbled to herself when finally sitting at her desk.

Michael had watched Xian as she took on the last three followers. She did indeed improve on her fighting technique but he noticed she was still hesitating when looking at people. *She still thinks she's fighting them and not the demons inside. I've got to come up with a way to break that mindset she's holding onto. Observation training should help with that. She needs to learn to recognize demon movements in human bodies; forget about focusing on their faces. Time to turn up the heat; she needs a closer glimpse into what is at stake.*

Michael knelt on his knees and began to pray. As he did he changed from the appearance of a human man to his true form reappearing almost instantly in the presence of God. Once there he requested if it was God's will, He'd show Xian in a dream what she needed to do. Show her just what the demons did to the human bodies they possess. Grant her the gift to look at a person and not see them as such, but as one who is controlled by a demon; a lost soul.

Later that evening, Michael met up with her and they hung out on the balcony of a vacant hotel room. The distance from the street was just far enough for Xian to see the people below. Michael instructed her to watch the way they moved. Not to focus on any one individual but to look at the movement of the crowd as a whole.

"Does anyone seem to be moving out of the ordinary to you?" He asked not taking his eyes off the streets below.

After a few minutes had passed and a deep sigh, he saw her sit more upright and lean toward the railing from the corner of his eye. Smiling he realized she spotted something.

"Tell me what you see."

"There just passing the pizza place, yellow t-shirt. He seems to walk a few steps then almost reappear a few feet further, but I don't see him actually walk there."

"What else?"

"Shadows moving quickly under the streetlights, trying hard to walk just outside their sphere of illumination on the sidewalks."

Nodding, Michael listened as she continued to point out others. By his count she had spotted all except for a few. He was impressed as well as relieved. This would make the next stage of her training a bit easier.

"Come on, let's go. Time for you to learn how to move the way they do and track their scent."

"They have a scent. I don't remember smelling anything when we fought them before?" Xian said following him back into the hotel room and down the hallway towards the stairwell.

"You weren't able to smell them before because you hadn't developed your skills much at that time. Yes they have a distinct scent, but very few humans can smell it. As man's prayers to God are like that of sweet smelling fragrances, these smell similar to that of rotting eggs I guess you could say; that mixed with a hint of sulfur."

Trying to prepare her nose for what she was sure would be a memorable experience in a bad way, Xian walked along in silence.

"The scent is only present when a person is possessed. The rotting is their flesh slowly decaying from the evil presence inside. The hint of sulfur is from the ash that covers the fallen whose heavenly bodies burned away during the fall, leaving behind the ugly shells they now are. When not possessing a human body, you will only smell a much stronger scent of sulfur."

When they reached the sidewalk, Michael explained that to move the way they did, she needed to focus on the place she wanted to go. Some she'll notice seemingly jumped greater distances than others. This was due to them learning how to move in a human body from having possessed it for a longer period of time. Those who were newly possessed, the fallen inside still hadn't learned how to make the body move at will. They still had to contend with the remaining will of the person.

"Come to me, based on what I just told you," Michael said before moving in a flash just over ten feet away from her.

Focusing on the spot in front of him, letting her eyes close halfway while losing focus on everything around her, Xian stepped forward in her mind. When the thought was complete, she stood grinning in front of Michael. Without saying a word, and face emotionless, he moved away from her, this time half a block ahead, backward.

"Okay, showoff. How do you expect me to move backward like that," she mumbled.

Deciding to just keep going forward and not be all fancy, Xian focused on the spot next to him and again at the end of the thought, she was looking up at him sideways. Figuring he would throw her a curve ball, Michael in one motion, scaled the single-story building next to them. Like a game of following the leader, Xian didn't even think of the direction, just focused on the destination. When she landed next to him on the rooftop, he moved towards the next building's roof, then the next until they had reached the fifth rooftop.

"You're a fast learner," Michael smiled at her. It was the first sign of emotion he displayed since they started this exercise. At that moment Xian felt her confidence soar a bit more.

"As you were following me, did you see anyone follow you?"

"Ah no I didn't actually, was a bit busy focusing on where I wanted to land."

Following his gaze to the street below, Xian then spotted about a dozen possessed moving along the sidewalk across the street from where they stood. Feeling her boost of recent confidence subside, she waited for him to tell her what to do.

"With your new learned skill, you're going to take them head on with one kill shot each. You'll have to move in quick succession so that people passing by don't notice anything out of the ordinary. Remember, they can't see you when you move this way, only feel maybe the force of the wind as you pass by."

After a nod from him, Xian was on the pavement below, taking out the first one. After the fourth, she developed a rhythm and picked up speed with each strike. Carreau watched as his minions were taken out one by one. He also watched Michael observing the desolation from across the street peering over the ledge of the building. Deciding he needed to shake Xian's confidence a bit, Carreau waited until she was finished with the last one then swooped down and brought her to a rooftop nearby. Instinctively she began to attack him. In three moves he was about to land a blow to her right arm, when Michael struck him from the side.

CHAPTER 8

Carreau thought he would at least get one strike in before Michael made his way to the party, but regardless of the early crasher, he was determined to shake Xian up a bit. Xian, still charged from the attacks down on the street, charged for Carreau's exposed chest. Easily he dodged her advance. She didn't really see him move; all she felt was her loss of balance while falling forward, followed by sounds of Michael and Carreau fighting at her back.

"Aren't you going to let her finish me off Michael?" Carreau taunted. Michael didn't respond, only blocked another of Carreau's sword strikes and then pushed him aside. Shielding Xian, who was now standing behind him taking in this new opponent, Michael stared at Carreau. He was no minion, she was certain of it. His speed was similar to Michaels, dressed in armor as if he was expecting some serious action. Then there was only the distinct smell of sulfur emanating from him.

"Is this the one we're supposed to be afraid of?" Carreau snickered trying to get a better look at Xian from around Michaels' shoulder.

"What brother, can't speak?"

Slowly Michael turned and placed an arm around Xian's waist, holding her tightly against his side. Never taking his eyes off Carreau, he lifted her off the rooftop, landing just at the opening of the alley below. Xian decided to keep quiet. If and when Michael wanted to talk about what just happened, she knew it would be in his good time. Deep in their own thoughts they made their way back to her place. Once inside, she handed him a glass of cold water. The only sounds other than the traffic below, was of them both gulping down the refreshing liquid.

Michael kept standing near the window with a full view of the city. After he was satisfied they were not going to have any company busting in, he let his shoulders drop and motioned for her to take a seat in the nearby chair. Xian held her breath, she knew he was about to say something she needed to take in. The information she assumed, that was going to give her another perspective on the journey ahead; attentively she waited.

"Satan has six generals, you can call them, that oversee the minions. Each has special abilities and territories or strongholds to be exact, Azazel, Beelzebub, Carreau, Dagon, Meresin and Verrine. The one you just met was Carreau; he hardens the hearts of men against Gods truth. It would appear that those were his minions we've been battling lately. I noticed him lurking around the first time they tried to attack you in daylight. Xian remembered the smirk on Michaels' face that day on the rooftop. She realized it was the result of him spotting Carreau. Azazel rules the deserts and dry places. Beelzebub is the ultimate prince all minions. Dagon the prince of the depths and wet places, undoubtedly you have seen his symbolism about, many people are unaware they even bear his mark. I'll point them out to you later. Then there's Meresin the prince of the air who controls the thunder and lightning. He also has the ability to cause fire and plagues. That's five, leaving Verrine; who tempts men with impatience and can motivate them to take action even if it is not of their free will. Each of them will take specific training to defeat."

Turning now to face her, he sat in the opposite chair and continued,

"The reason I didn't engage Carreau in conversation was because he has the ability to tempt you with lies about God. I didn't want him to plant seeds of doubt in your mind about your gifts. I couldn't take the chance of him destroying all the confidence your hard work has built up. If he ever sees one spec of uncertainty in you when you try to take him on, he will feed it until it consumes you. Granted he can fight, but his mouth is really his weapon. Your skills get better each day, but you must be able to block out cunning words also, especially if you are to defeat Carreau."

Nodding to show she understood, Xian asked,

"Just how do I block out his words? Is there some trick to it?"

Pointing to her chest he said,

"The spark inside needs to grow until it fills you. Your faith must be so grounded in God that nothing and no one can shake you loose from it. Every time you hold that sword and the blade appears, every time you look at something others think are fairy tales, you must remember that it is all real. That your beliefs are all based on truth. This is how you'll keep grounded. Holding onto this will also make you grow stronger even when your physical body feels at its weakest."

He watched her lean back in her chair and process what he'd just said. Not wanting to lose the momentum of her training he added,

"Take it as a compliment that Satan has sent his general after you instead of just minions. I know for sure more will be watching us so from now on; we will train indoors, only going out to get in some target practice. You will, however, not use your full potential outside. I don't want anyone else to know just how skilled you've become.

I will train with you on techniques to sharpen all your skills," he said as he too leaned back in his chair.

Seeing her slight concern for his wellbeing, he smiled and said,

"Don't worry; you're no match for me even on your best day. Besides I have some secrets skills of my own."

Once he saw her relax knowing she couldn't hurt him he continued,

"Out of all of them, Carreau and Verrine are the ones you need to handle by using less physical strength. Like I said Carreau you pretty much have to ignore his big mouth and as for Verrine, you have to beat him by developing more patience. Yeah, we both know that's an area you really need to work on," he chuckled as she shot him a look, only to smile and nod in agreement.

"The rest pretty much will fall by fighting them, using all the techniques you will learn. Never for one minute underestimate your abilities. Forget about if they're bigger or faster than you. Trust your training and most of all have faith in your source."

Slowly Xian stretched in the chair then got up to look out the window. The moon was bright and the city teamed with life. Gazing now at her own reflection in the window she asked,

"So do I have it right that you will not be personally going up against any of these generals? I'm the one who pretty much will be doing the deed?"

"Yes you have it right, but you will only go up against them when I know you're good and ready. Until then I'm here to shield you from them. The minions we can agree, you can handle alone. Still we are together in this until the day we aren't."

His words did double duty in her heart, comforting and piercing at the same time. Her emotions were starting to get the best of her. It had been a long day and the revelations of the last few hours were starting to take a toll on her. Without saying a word, Michael pushed her in the direction of her bathroom. She understood and nodded. A good shower and her bed were what her body needed right now. When he heard her pull back the shower curtain and step into the flow of water, Michael went into her kitchen. Spotting some leftover take out he proceeded to heat up a variety of combinations, half eaten in the fridge. His body was demanding nourishment and he was sure Xian must be starving too.

Once she was dressed in shorts and a tank top, they ate the food in near silence. Xian was happy for the quiet and let her mind drift to memories of carefree summers when she was a child; playing with cousins and friends like there was no tomorrow. Michael watched her through quick glances trying not to make her uncomfortable. He could tell she was thinking of something pleasant from her smiling eyes. He too let himself think of his life before the fall. He and his brothers were also happy to just serve; then it all changed. His face became hard with the memory and Xian caught it.

Not knowing what to say, she thanked him for making a meal from the scraps in the kitchen and all his patience with her. She went on to tell him how she would be lost without him, anything she thought that would make him smile.

"I will die giving it my all Michael," she said watching him with tear filled eyes.

The sincerity in her words made the corners of his mouth turn upward. He waited until she was asleep before surveying outside one last time. After an hour of scanning the area, satisfied there were no real threats, he decided to head home. Anyways, he was comforted by the fact that her building was surrounded by a host of angels, something he made a mental note to tell her later. He figured it would ease her fear of being alone. With one more glance at her bedroom window, just in time to see two angels entering through the nearby walls, he shot into the night's sky.

The soft sounds of Xian's snoring created an out of rhythm mix against the city's beat below. Standing on either side of her bed, the two angels posted guard for the night. Senses still heightened by the day's events, she stirred and fought to open her eyes. All she managed to do was pry them open a quarter of the way. Straining to focus on a silhouette to her left, she lifted her head a few inches off the pillow. Words formed in her throat remained trapped as her mouth refused to open. By the third blink she felt a presence on her right shoulder nudging her back down on the bed. Too exhausted to resist, she closed her eyes and drifted off to sleep as a peaceful feeling enveloped her.

Soon she was floating above the Earth looking down, taking in the beauty of its whites and blues. Turning to look for Michael, who she thought had brought her back up in the air to spectate, she began to feel a panic coming on with the realization he was nowhere in sight.

"Don't be afraid, you will not fall," said a voice from, Xian assumed, the angel that suddenly stood in front of her.

"It was Michael who asked that you be shown just what is at stake, how important the task given to you is. Our Father has sent me to fill you in."

Peeling her eyes off him now, she looked again at the Earth below her feet. No longer was it white and blue, it was now engulfed in red and orange flames. Dark shadows moved all over the surface as well as in the air. Screaming sounds of varying pitches and volume rose up towards her. As her eyes widened, the angel said,

"This is an image of what is to come after your task is complete. A certain future you are to save as many as possible from experiencing. Our Father never wanted mankind to endure such suffering; it is the intended end for Satan and his followers. However, there are many who refuse to hear and accept Gods truth. Understand that though you can help to save many, not everyone will be saved," with an outstretched arm he continued,

"Sadly this reality is what awaits those that have turned away from Gods offer of eternal life."

Tears threatened to flood Xian's face as she took in the sight below her; images of all the people she knew came to mind. Many she knew did not accept Christ and the thought of them ending up in this reality tore at her core.

"Take courage in knowing that the Father has provided you with everything you need to complete your tasks. You are being trained in spiritual warfare by one of his most trusted."

Seeing her eyes brighten at the thought of Michael and a smile begin to form on her face, he continued,

"Your feelings for him are noted and understandable given your female human emotions. You have accepted him as he truly is and despite the fact that you are not really compatible, you care for him all the same."

Seeing embarrassment now on her face as she tried to shield it with her hands, he touched them, pushing them away.

"You have nothing to feel embarrassed or ashamed about. Your love for him is part of the tangible reference you require to see the journey to the end; use it."

Xian now looked right at his face. He had dark brown eyes, nothing particularly special about his features. She could have sworn he look a little like the owner of her favorite café she often got breakfast and coffee from on her way to work.

"If it helps, know that in the only way he can, he loves you too. He will do everything within his power to protect you. This is the way he shows his love."

Nodding and with a forced smile, she turned her gaze again towards the fiery blaze below.

After tossing in bed for the past thirty minutes, Michael just stared up at the ceiling. It was pointless to try and not address the issue any longer. Some of the side effects of this human form were suddenly plaguing him. Feelings that never before made themselves apparent, were oozing into his conscious thoughts; shaking his head was not making them go away either. It was absurd to even consider, she is a human and he an angel. He knows she has strong feelings for him; he sensed them every time they were near each other. Not sure how long he would be in this current form, he didn't see the point in even trying to find out where it all could lead. He just assumed he would be going back to Heaven once she had completed her task; things would go back to the way they were, sort of.

"I have a clear path to take," he mumbled to himself, "and trying out some inter-species relationship by human standards is definitely not a pit stop on this path."

Not entirely convinced by what he just uttered, he rolled over and took deep breaths to help relax his mind, willing sleep to come to him. It wasn't working.

"Enough of these maddening thoughts about the two of us, I really need to be free of this flesh suit for a while. I feel like I'm losing my grip on reality," he said aloud in the empty room.

With a long groan he took flight in his true form until he was high above the Earth. He had no particular destination in mind, just wanted to feel like his self for a change. Seeing a few of his brothers off in the distance, he headed towards them and learned they were standing watch over a revival being held by missionaries below. Just being near them gave Michael a boost he desperately needed. He gazed below at those in attendance of the revival and smiled as many opened their hearts and minds to Gods truth. It was a great thing to see, compared to all the darkness he faced each day. Instinctively he began to speak and point toward the crowd as if to show Xian.

Realizing it was no use he left the other angels and headed up. As fast as he could soar he barreled his way towards Heaven. Once granted access into Gods presence, he opened himself up exposing all his concerns. Almost immediately he felt a burst of energy fill him. With clearer understanding now, he stayed bowed until he was no longer in God's presence. With a long look around Heaven, he took into himself every inch he could. Etching to memory all he saw. A renewed sense of love and gratitude overpowered him as he slowly descended back to his earthly body.

Morning brought clear bright skies to Miami. Xian awoke feeling more determined to do her best; her dream still fresh in her mind. Michael found himself staring in the bathroom mirror, taking in his earthly appearance as if for the first time. A growing sense of relief crept in his heart, knowing now that he was not losing it. While Richard felt as if maybe his luck was going to change today. Smiling he hoped it had to do with Jenny. The possibility of being with her was really getting him to see things in a better light. Something good had to come out of all the misery his life had been filled with so far. Jenny sure was something good he wanted to sample. Meanwhile, Jenny took extra care in selecting her outfit for the day. Sexy thoughts raced through her mind as she picked out a matching lace underwear set. Admiring the pieces on her frame in her full-length mirror, she wondered if Richard would find them as fabulous as she did.

    As Xian, Richard and Jenny almost in unison exited their apartments, headed for work, Michael stood guard over the route Xian took every day. Today she looked particularly appealing to him.

    Okay, you're definitely going to have to get a handle on these human emotions, he thought, *focus on the crowd and skies above. All you need is for the enemy to catch you drooling over her; no way are they to find out your judgment may be clouded by human emotions.*

CHAPTER 9

Xian was having a hard time getting the dream of Satan's plans out of her head. No matter how she tried to distract herself, the magnitude of it all threatened to consume her. She just wanted a safe place to escape, even if just for a little while. Balancing her daily life with the new one which took over her nights was taking its toll. Dark circles had begun to form under her eyes resulting in some of her coworker's giving weary looks whenever she was around. A few had already experienced short outbursts from her over the simplest things; her patience was wearing thinner by the day. Xian knew she couldn't keep this pace much longer.

Michael had noticed it too. He tried to give her as much time to sleep as he could, but there was just a lot she still needed to learn. Something was going to have to give and her job was certainly the only logical choice. Financially she would be taken care of; he had more than enough means to see to that. Convincing her to take some time off or even walk away from work for an extended period, he wasn't sure she'd just go for. Either way, he had to get more training time in with her; nothing like the present for one to go cold turkey. The next time they were together, he planned to approach the subject.

That opportunity came rather quickly. He met up with Xian at her place an hour after she got there later the same day. As usual he'd scouted the area around her apartment for anyone that may have been following her. He also wanted to give her a chance to clear her head of the day before taking her to train. His head could use some clearing too. Something was different about him since returning from Heaven. Stronger emotions kept plaguing him whenever he thought of Xian. Having them now thrown in the mix by God was definitely going to make his situation even more challenging. He was accustomed to following clean and decisive instructions. Never had any past interactions with humans involved feelings that blurred everything. Regardless, he was not going to let anything disappoint God; he trusted him with this assignment. How hard could it be?

Xian walked straight to her bed upon getting home. She could barely keep her balance as she walked and undressed along the way. Turning she fell backward, exhaling as her weight became supported by the firm mattress. With seemingly just two deep breaths, she was knocked out. For once in a long time she didn't dream. Her mind welcomed the chance to shut down, while her tired body lay still on the bed. Just over forty-five minutes had passed when a knock on her front door interrupted her slumber. She blinked hard to try and focus her eyes. Fumbling for a robe hanging behind the bedroom door, she put it on while wondering who it could be. Michael would soon be by, but he was not one to use the door. Peeking through the keyhole, she looked straight into his eyes; weird he seemed to be looking right through her.

"Since when did you start using the door," she asked side stepping so he could come in.

"Thought I'd try to act more human; adjust my actions to blend in better whenever we go out and stuff."

Looking at him a bit confused, Xian headed back towards her room to put on some clothes. Realizing that he'd barely said anything else since arriving; she hurried with her sneakers and joined him in the living room space. He was staring at her, his usual intense gaze seemed a bit softer, as if he had a question formulating behind his eyes.

"What?" she asked plopping in a side chair opposite him.

A deafening silence lasted another minute before Michael leaned forward without taking his eyes off her, in a low voice he asked,

"How are you feeling? You look tired."

"I'll be okay," she said trying to fake a smile.

Not buying it, Michael continued to hold her gaze as he leaned back in the sofa.

"I know the pace we've been going has started to wear you down physically and mentally. Your world has been put in a blender and there is a lot for you to sort out." Pausing to watch for any reactions from her, he waited a bit before continuing, to be effective in this fight, you're going to need to be at the top of your game. You need to take a break from work. All your financial needs will be met."

The slight sign of relief in her eyes and relaxing of her shoulders surprised him. Maybe the strain had already broken her resolve. Either way he was happy that at least this didn't turn into a drawn out debate. Shadows from the buildings outside were slowing casting themselves along the side of her face. She looked so beautiful at that moment. A sudden tightening in his chest caught him off guard. To disguise his uneasiness, Michael shifted his weight in the sofa.

"How much notice do you need to give your boss?"

"Ah I don't know, I guess at least two weeks. So, how exactly will my financial needs be met? Will I still get to keep my apartment?"

"I'll be taking care of them and you can keep your apartment until it no longer becomes a viable choice," said Michael, still looking at her face for any signs to tell what she may be thinking. She wasn't giving much away. Maybe he should let her just rest tonight. He'd been drilling her pretty hard and it was important that she find the rhythm that would be her new normal. A change of pace might be a just what she needed.

"I'll order delivery tonight. You really ought to get some rest; turn in early. We'll make up in practice tomorrow," he smiled hoping to disguise his discomfort.

With a grateful smile, Xian let her head fall on the back of the chair as her body slide forward a bit.

"Whatever you choose is fine by me. I just want something tasty and hot."

By this time Michael was already looking through the take-out menus she had in a kitchen drawer. Settling on the one from the dinner just up the block, he called in an order for them both and then returned to the sofa. By this time she was sleeping again; her breathing heavy and deep. He sat back on the sofa across from her and stared, taking in every inch as if for the first time. He noticed the curls of her hair, lines of her face, slowly going down her body. The sight of her was stirring deep emotions, his pulse was speeding up and now his mouth had become dry, making it harder to swallow. He saw how human men acted when overtaken by a woman, he was no human man. Worse he was an angel given human emotions. Their intensity was magnified over a thousand times for him. It took a great effort for him to focus and not act on them. Michael knew Xian found him attractive from the first time they met. It was he who had drawn the line, set the boundaries. As far as she knew, nothing had changed.

Yet he knew and felt different.

His new mandate would require balancing his role as a teacher and protector with that of friend and lover. Tact was in order and he was out of his league with the latter part of this mix. He needed help in the worse way; he needed Marcus. Yes Marcus would know how he should handle things since he has spent so much time on earth amongst humans. Mentally Michael decided to go pay him a visit later that evening, there was much he had to understand. Before Michael could dwell further on his emotional issues, there was a knock on the door.

The food was delivered by a young guy wearing a baseball cap with the dinner's logo on it. The exchange of money and food went quickly as the young man thanked Michael for the tip and hurried down the hall towards the stairs. Noting he was just a harmless human, Michael closed the door and set the food out on the dining table.

Xian was still sleeping soundly when he approached her. Instinctively, Michael's right hand pushed back a lock of curls that had fallen across her face. The tips of his fingers gently brush her cheek, causing her to stir. Her face moved in towards his fingers, moving up and down to maintain the contact. Longingly his eyes focused on her lips, and then quickly his gaze was on her eyes, which were slowly beginning to open. Using his speed, Michael walked over to the dining table pushing the forks around, pretending as if he was never near her.

"Time to eat," he said without taking his eyes off the table.

"Oh wow, I'm sorry for dosing off on you like that," Xian said as she stretched her arms above her head, walking towards the table. "It smells so good, what'd you order?"

"For you, I got meatloaf with mashed potatoes and vegetables. For me a double stacked cheeseburger and fries with lemon meringue pie for desert."

Noticing her raised eyebrows when he mentioned the pie, Michael quickly added, "and yes I did get an extra slice for myself so you don't have to share yours."

They said grace and with a big smile Xian dove in. She was famished; all the exercising was making her burn calories like crazy. After savoring the second mouthful, she held up her head and leaned back in the chair. Michael was making his way through his burger, periodically picking up a French fry every other bite. The only sounds in the room were that of the two of them eating and the low buzz of traffic in the streets below. Lost in his thoughts, Michael wondered if she was aware of the moment he stood over her. If she did, she was hiding it well. Her only focus seemed to be the plate in front of her. Pushing the thoughts aside, he worked on finishing his food, trying to act normal.

Aware of the tension emanating from Michael on her left, Xian acted as if nothing else in the world existed but the food she was chowing down. He seemed a bit off to her. The stares were more intense than usual. Sometimes she could swear she saw desire in his eyes, but that couldn't be right since he'd made it all too clear where the lines were in their relationship. Before she woke, she could feel him near, touching her cheek, she was certain of it. But when she opened her eyes, he was across the room. *That means nothing though with his speed capabilities.* Now sitting at the table pretending to have another normal meal, she couldn't dispel the little knot in her stomach telling her something's changed.

While they were eating desert, Michael explained that he needed to go and see Marcus afterward. He suggested she get to bed and rest up and that she needn't worry, she was being watched over while he was away. Happy for the opportunity to curl up under her bed covers, Xian smiled and nodded while swallowing down the last piece of her pie. By the time she cleared the table and turned around from the kitchen, he was gone. Letting out a long sigh, she checked the front door was locked and made her way to the bathroom. A good hot shower and then sleep was all she could think of. *Whatever he's dealing with, he'll tell me soon enough.* With that she turned on the hot water and prepared to enjoy her night off.

When Michael arrived at Marcus's store, it was already closed. Knowing he would most likely be somewhere in one of the back rooms he used as living space, Michael took the side alley leading to a private entrance. Before he was within three steps of the door, it opened. Locking the door behind him, he followed Marcus down a dimly lit hallway towards his makeshift living and dining area. After letting the much-weathered fabric sofa envelop him, Michael broke the silence,

"I need your help."

"Oh?" said Marcus, turning away from television so that he could face Michael.

"My orders changed recently and I'm having a little trouble adjusting."

Marcus didn't speak; he just looked intently at the figure in front of him. He couldn't recall a time when Michael was never in control of himself. Shifting his weight and leaning forward, staring harder at Michaels face he slowly said,

"If I didn't know better, I would swear your face looks like a man with woman problems."

The words resulted with Michaels eyes quickly locking onto those of Marcus. Not wanting to appear weak, yet needing desperately to get a release from all the tension building up, Michael exhaled then nodded his head. Marcus leaned back into his chair rubbing his chin. With pressed lips he nodded, eyes narrowing as if struck by a sudden revelation.

"You're to be more than Xian's protector, aren't you?"

"Yes and these new levels of emotions I feel are making me uneasy. I already know she has feelings for me but both of us can't have our heads filled with clouds. There's still a lot of training to do and if Satan were to even suspect anything, he'd use it against us."

"Do you trust The Father's wisdom in changing your orders?"

"Of course I do. It was just so much simpler with me training, she obeying and then she'd go off with the man meant for her."

"I see nothing about that idea being changed."

"What? I'm an archangel Marcus, my duty is to fight not be tied to a woman."

"Your duty is to do Gods will and who better than you to have her back? You know all too well who and what she is up against. I can tell you my friend; receiving free love from a human surpasses that of anyone who is merely loyal to you."

With uncertainty still in his eyes, Michael stared towards the television screen. After a few moments he stood up and started to pace, it seemed with each step the room was closing in on him more and more.

Marcus words brought him to an abrupt halt.

"He chose you because he knows you'd give your life for her. That is the type of man she needs. No human can give her that level of devotion; love. The changes in your body are all chemical and just like all other training you've mastered, this one will be without exception."

"I don't know what to do around her. I have such a strong desire to hold her close. My mind becomes flooded with all these images and I…" he trailed off, ending in a long sigh.

"You've seen couples together, so I know you got a pretty good understanding of what goes on between a woman and man when the fires' lit. Just go with it when that time comes. She trusts you and that, believe it or not, will make this transition in your relationship much easier for both of you."

Scratching at the back of his neck, Michael gave Marcus a small genuine smile. Deep inside he just needed to hear what he was feeling was normal and that he hadn't lost his true self to these new desires. He needed fresh air. Needed distance from the city if only for a moment. Sensing his restlessness, Marcus turned back to face the television, surfing the channels.

"I'm here whenever you need to talk. Don't forget to lock the door on your way out."

Taking the queue to leave, Michael grunted as he headed for the back door. The sudden night air felt good in his lungs as he quickened his steps going further into the dark alley. When sure no one could see him, he bolted into the air. His body soared above the clouds; every so often he would spin himself as he climbed upward. After traveling for over two minutes, he stopped and looked out into the dark space. The blue earth below him shimmered like a glass marble. It was a sight he never tired of seeing. Hours passed as he just drifted along with no particular destination in mind. With his thoughts slowing settling and a plan formulated, Michael slowly smiled because he felt in control again. Alright then, if I'm going to fulfill my duty, I need to Xian ready because there is no way I want Satan to use my feelings for her against us. She needs to be able to mask her emotions as I do because once I let my true feelings show to her, I'll have a giddy female on my hands. After closing his eyes and shaking his head, he descended almost as fast back towards her apartment.

When he arrived, she was almost totally covered by her blanket. The moonlight was casting a bright beam along the wall above her beds headboard. He signaled to the guardian angels he would continue the watch and once they had left he gave into the pull and laid next to her. She smelled like fresh fruit, undoubtedly from one of the many bottles shower gel stockpiled in her bathroom. Before he knew what was happening, he had her nestled against him, instinctively her head adjusted on his chest. Once he realized she hadn't awakened, he stared out the window into the night's sky. Being near her calmed him, making him feel even more invincible and strangely vulnerable as well.

CHAPTER 10

The morning sky gave Michael renewed energy as streaks of orange and red crept across the sky. Xian had slept soundly all through the night and he contemplated going into the living room versus staying next to her in the bed. Deciding to remain where he was and get things out in the open sooner than later once she woke, he held up his arms as she moved trying to get in a new comfortable position. This time she had positioned most of her upper body onto his chest; head slowly adjusting trying to conform his chest to the contours of her face. Her body became suddenly stiff; she was awake.

"Good morning sleepy head," he almost whispered "you slept soundly all night."

Trying to wet her dry throat, Xian swallowed hard not sure if to move or stay put. *What in the world happened last night? I know I was tired and my mind is blank. How is it I'm waking up with my head glued to his chest? Oh lord this chest feels so...snap out of it girl and just slowly roll off,* she thought to herself.

Now sitting up facing him she asked with her head turned looking at him sideways,

"Ah what did I miss? The last thing I remembered was crawling into bed after a good hot shower. You had already left and ah, did you come back or something?"

"I did but it was a long time after you had fallen asleep. Nothing out of the ordinary happened."

"Hmm, well you and me in bed together I'd say was something out of the ordinary, wouldn't you?"

Sighing he sat up so his back was leaning against the headboard. He felt like pudding inside, not the hardened warrior he was known for. Why can't I get a grip on these emotions yet? This close proximity is too much; I got to get out this bed. Yeah walking around may help calm my raw nerves. Realizing she was still waiting on his answer, he fumbled with the blanket now entangled around his feet as he attempted to make his escape. Once free and standing several feet away near the window he said with his back to her,

"My orders have changed. I am not only to train and protect you, God has decided that I am to also be you soul mate, for lack of a better description."

The only sound he could hear was that of his pulse beating loudly in his ears. Then there was the rustling of bedding followed by her slow footsteps stopping just behind him. He could feel her eyes boring into his back; feel her energy just within reach.

"Are you alright with this change?" she asked softly, "I know this isn't really your thing and before you firmly corrected me for any feelings I was developing for you."

"Honestly I'm struggling a bit with all of the waves that attack me. I'm trying to figure out how to be all those things to you and not mess up our fighting relationship. When I train you, there will be times I'll need to push and be hard. I just want you to know it doesn't mean I don't care. Ah man this is harder than I imagined it would be. You must think me to be pretty weak now?"

"The opposite, you're stronger than I thought. It takes a lot for a man to open up and since you're not really all man I can only guess this must be a real wrench in your wheel. Look its cool, I'm really kinda' glad, you know? I mean you know I have feelings for you and now you're having the same for me, so we're good, right?"

Turing to face her finally, he looked into her hopeful eyes. She was so beautiful with her curls framing her face, her top snuggly fitting all her curves and her pants clinging just right; the visual wasn't helping.

"Yes we're good," he managed to get out while turning her around by the shoulders, shoving her towards the bathroom, "get dressed for work, we'll have breakfast before you go in and let your boss know you need to take a leave of absence."

Without any resistance she did as she was told. Michael knew that the leave would be permanent but figured he'd explain that when necessary later down the road. He thought of food and some training techniques for Xian, anything to stop him from following her into the bathroom. *Just how is this going to work? Are we getting married before something physical happens between us? Marriage! Can I even get married? Ahh, more stuff added to my full plate*, he thought as he went into the living room.

Xian had been able to give her notice as soon as she got to work. To her delight she was able to start her leave right away. The company had an influx of college interns and her workload was a great place for them to start since other departments in the company were too busy and not wanting to train anyone at the moment. By the time she had divided the workload, it was late in the afternoon. Figuring she'd spend the next hour or so clearing her desk, she first made her rounds to coworkers letting them know she'd be out of office for a while. A part of her would miss this familiar piece of her life. She knew while making her way back to her desk to collect her things, there was a high possibility that she wasn't coming back. The reality that her life was forever changed really hit her at that moment.

The short elevator ride down to the lobby evoked tears in her eyes, which she blinked quickly away, plastering a big smile on her face as she said goodbye to some colleagues waiting to enter the elevator. She was so wrapped up in her thoughts; she hadn't noticed Michael waiting for her near the entrance of the parking garage. Not sure what to do or say when she got near, she just smiled as genuinely as possible and said hello. Michael smiled back briefly, took her small boxed belongings and walked in silence towards her car.

Once inside he told her after a quick stop by her place for her to change, they were going to start training on her ability to detect the changes in energy around her. If she was going to be on the offensive in this war, she must be able to see the enemy coming. He explained that the technique would also help her to guard her emotions which could be used against her in a fight. She had to learn to always appear unmoved regardless of the situation; fear and doubt would not only paralyze her but also give opponents something to feed their powers with.

"Understand,' he said as they drove along, "they are only as strong as you allow them to be. From your fear and doubt, they develope a sense of boldness, they work on your mind which cripples you from the inside, without ever having to land a blow physically. This is Satan's most used form of attack; he and his minions."

Since her apartment was heavily guarded, Michael took her to the rooftop to train. For the next few days at least she would be doing more mental training than physical anyways. Standing back to back he instructed her to walk forward ten steps, close her eyes and keep completely still. By this time he had walked the same amount of steps in the opposite direction.

"Now I want you to count to five out loud and point with either hand where you feel I am. You can't look to find me; you must rely on your senses only. Understand?"

"Yes."

As Xian began to count, Michael moved about, standing still whenever she got to the number four. To his delight, she was pretty close to accurate the first few times.

"Take calming deep breaths and focus on the flow of energy around you. All around you energy is in motion, where do you sense a disruption of that energy? "

She pointed to a large pole sticking out the roof.

"Good try but is that object itself giving off energy?"

"No," she said with slight disappointment.

"Remember, every living thing gives off distinct energy, either it is a part of Satan's evil energy or pure powerful love from God. Start counting again and focus; find me."

Xian slowly counted this time and with each number her eyes seemed to see shapes. She squeezed them tight to be certain they were closed. With her head turning from side to side she stopped with her neck turned as far as it'd go to her right. Just out of the farthest corner she saw little specs of bluish white. With a small smirk forming at the corners of her mouth, she lifted her right hand and point towards Michael. He broke out into a big grin as he nodded.

"Good, now try again."

This time he waited until she was about to say the number five before moving to the opposite side of the roof he had just been. She pointed straight at him. They continued the exercise for over an hour, each time he moved faster and faster. Each time she found him. To turn up the challenge a notch, he gently tossed small stones at her, which he instructed she was to swat away so as not to get hit by them.

As he expected, the first few hit their target, but after a while she was able to knock them off course. Soon she was reaching out towards the approaching stones, anticipating their path. Satisfied she was ready to up the skill level he reached for a pair of practice sticks and still with her eyes closed, he slowly came at her with strikes. The clicking sound of the sticks filled the air around them, its rhythm all Xian was focusing on, letting the busy streets below become a distant hum in her ears.

After almost four hours of training, Michael decided she had enough for the night. Besides, her stomach was really growling and the mixed aromas of food coming from the streets below were making it hard for him to concentrate. He marveled at how he didn't need to sleep yet his human form almost always wanted to be feed. Not wanting to get trapped inside her apartment so soon, he decided they should go out to eat. He waited patiently as she changed, out front watching the skyline from the living room window. Not much activity which he wasn't sure if it made him happy or concerned. Though there were angels patrolling which most likely was keeping the minion spies at a distance.

Xian stood near the front door shaking her head as she said with a laugh,

"At least you could pretend to need to take a shower, instead of using your juice and changing your clothes."

Smiling he looked down at himself, so accustomed to just changing appearance with a thought he chimed in,

"You know maybe I'll start doing it your way. You seem to really enjoy the array of shower gels in your collection. However, I'd prefer something less flowery."

Both laughed and proceeded out the building. Michael decided they should celebrate her accomplishments tonight during training and go have dinner on the beach. He was in the mood for seafood, to which Xian excitingly agreed. They took her car and literally let the sea breeze blow through their hair as they crossed over onto Miami Beach. As they drove along seemingly without a care in the world, overhead flew a dozen demons zigzagging their flight, cautious not to be spotted by Michael. Their orders were to test Xian's abilities and report any improvements of weaknesses to Carreau. He had invested too much into Bishop Strickman and his congregation to let her mess things up with little resistance. Honestly, if she destroys a couple hundred of my minions it will only make me look better before Satan when I obliterate her. When I'm done, there will be little to bury......I see cremation of the few remains I'm going to leave as the only option for her friends and family he thought to himself as he made his way to Strickman's church. Tonight there were several meetings and rehearsals going on. All of which provided a great opportunity for him to release some of the demons waiting in his office storage to possess. Grinning now, he flew faster not wanting to miss one single vessel, especially those lingering in the parking lot outside. They were always such easy pickings.

Dinner turned out to be just what Xian needed. They chose to be seated outside the cozy restaurant in a corner booth facing the ocean. Though they couldn't see much except the cresting of waves crashing along the shoreline under the bright moonlight, the rhythmic sounds of the sea was a relaxing backdrop. Michael purposely kept the conversation light, even though Xian's eyes and facial expressions sometimes showed she was thinking of deeper thoughts. He just didn't want to go down the emotion road at that moment. She was good about it though and didn't press, instead she complimented the food and then how each new fighting technique gave her more confidence. She was even amazing herself at how easily it all was coming to her. While still talking about training, she suddenly said in mid-sentence without turning her head,

"Do you smell that?" she asked of the slight hint of sulfur in the air.

"Yes. They're trying to stay downwind of us but the breeze is getting turned around by this overhanging tarp. Continue eating, they will look for bodies to possess then attack once we leave."

They sat at the table for another twenty minutes then casually got up to leave after paying the check. Letting her walk ahead, Michael quickly scanned everyone within their path all way to Xian's parked car. He spotted twelve, mostly male except for three.

"Alright, let's see put your new skills to the test. You'll take point and I'll backup if you get in trouble. How many have you spotted?"

"Hmm I count eight so far."

"Good but there are still more between us and the car. Give me your final count as soon as you have it."

Xian had walked along the beach instead of the sidewalk, hoping to draw the fight away from an audience. The closer to the shore she got, the darkness became a great blanket covering them from any curious eyes and smart-phones ready to upload a video. Once out of view from the public, three were circling her. They looked as if sizing her up and while laughing as to how small she was, Xian reached for her sword and with four quick rotations of her body, stood back where she started laughing back at them. By this time, each was clutching their chest while dropping to their knees with a look of what just happened on their faces.

This spurred on low growl coming from her left as four more attacked one after the other. Their weapons were broken glass bottles, pieces of scrap wood and a metal rod. The sound of her sword as she blocked them drifted up into the night's sky. Michael stood off to the side observing, making sure she was in control of the situation and that there were no unwanted human onlookers hiding in the darkness. Patiently the others waited for a chance at her, but all too soon was that time upon them, only to feel the blade of her sword separate them from the human vessels they were temporarily occupying.

      The last three were the most skilled of the bunch. Yet they were no match for Xian. By this time Michael could tell she was toying with them. Using them as practice dummies, perfecting her attacking and defensive moves; checking her balance was always sure. She glanced over to see him looking at her as if saying end this already. So she did just that.

CHAPTER 11

Every day Xian is taking on more possessed. Michael finds himself pretty much just standing in the wings as she gets more control over her developing skills. At times he notices that she gets a bit over confident, underestimating the abilities of her opponents. A star at a fallen body held too long, resulting in a surprise blow to her blind side. She still used too much of her natural vision to keep up the speed and awareness necessary for really large numbers.

"Stop showboating already. You're going to get hurt if you keep using your eyes alone on them," he shouted.

Letting out a loud grunt, Xian settled herself and focused on the dark energy they exuded. Closing her eyes really made a difference as she was able to sense and see with a much wider range. Her speed also increased as a result. Seemed like lately the attackers came at her in larger numbers; adding at least a dozen to the number more than the group before. She could tell things were really getting serious, even for her current level of abilities, the numbers felt a bit much. Making a mental note to ask Michael about this, she took a series of side steps, slashing as she did at the almost single file of bodies rushing her. *Seriously, is he just gonna stand there and watch.* As if he could read her mind, Michael shouted,

"Yup, they're all yours. Now show me all you got."

With that she tapped deep into herself and felt a surge of energy escape her, hitting the nearest body and propelling it like a fast rolling bowling ball knocking down several people in its path. Michael's face was plastered with a big grin. His relentless training methods were paying off. *Just the right nudge to her ego gets the results we need. Hmm so now I know just how to flip your switch,* he thought.

Nothing like a good workout to build up a monster appetite; today was no exception to the other ones of late. They had become a staple at the local dinner; always picking the same seats and by now had eaten everything on the standard menu at least twice. The way Xian felt at the moment though, called for the daily special which just happened to be pot roast. Even Michael was eager to try it as they wantonly stared over at the plates in front of the patrons at a nearby table. While waiting on their order, Xian decided to get some answers.

"So are you always going to just stand around while I do all the fighting?"

"You're still in training. So yes, I'll be observing nearby until I see you're ready for some real action."

"What I've seen so far doesn't qualify as real action to you?" She said leaning back in her seat with a wide-eyed expression.

"Remember the office building that was housing a group of demons waiting for bodies to possess?"

"Yeah I remember. What about them?"

"The day you can clear that many possessed without hardly breaking a sweat, that day is the day I say you're ready for some real action. Look, what you've been up against so far are just foot soldiers. Like any army, there are the ones that attack first to weaken the enemy, only to be followed by those that finish the deal."

He let the words sink in; downing the glass of water he was holding. Noticing she was going over it all from the distant stare in her eyes, he checked out the windows for anyone lurking around. Satisfied that there was no immediate threat, he looked back at her. She was still lost in thought, only brought back to the present by the arrival of their two steaming plates of homemade goodness. Almost simultaneously they both dug in, stuffing their faces as if it was the first meal they'd had in more than a day. Nothing else was said until they were walking out the dinner, stretching and rubbing their rounded guts. Sleep was making its appearance in Xian's eyes as they walked the short distance to her apartment.

The moonlight made her look so inviting to Michael as they walked across the intersection. Not too many people were on the streets yet, which gave him quite an unobstructed view of her. His mind wondered and he felt warmth creep up his body; his face felt hot suddenly. Xian walked along clueless to Michael's predicament. Her thoughts had gone back to what he'd said about those she'd faced so far only being basically grunts; not the most skilled fighters. When they were a few feet from her apartment door she turned to him and asked,

"Do you think I'll really be able to clear that large a number alone?"

Looking down at her perplexed expression made him get all fuzzy inside. She looked so vulnerable and helpless, quite different from the sword-wielding warrior in training he'd witnessed just a few hours ago. Before he realized what his hand was doing, he tilted her head up a little more as he bent down to plant a kiss on her forehead. As he lifted his face he whispered,

"I have no doubt."

Not sure how to react, she fumbled with her keys and opened the door. Flipping on the light switch she dropped her keys on the dining table and began to loosen her hair. It was damp from sweat and all she wanted to do was wash it and let her body brush scrub away all the negative residue left behind from her fighting. She'd been so set on getting in the shower; she'd forgotten Michael was still there, only remembering when he closed the bathroom door behind him. Face half covered in shampoo, she peeked to see if he'd come in or just closed the door while staying on the other side of it.

"Michael is that you?"

"Yes," he mumbled almost embarrassed to speak," do you mind if I watch you?"

Not sure just where this was headed, but remembering he was still trying to get a grip on his emotions, she told him it was okay in the most nonchalant tone she could muster. He leaned back on the counter top as she continued to wash her hair then start on her body. Xian tried to ignore his intent gaze and now wished she'd opted for the printed shower curtain instead of the plain clear one. Realizing it was pointless to try and hide, she pretended he wasn't so close and hummed herself a melody. The water felt good as it beat on her shoulders and back. She just stood there for a moment, and then the moment passed. While her eyes were still closed, she saw his energy begin to fill the small bathroom space. The light blue light was moving towards her. Her eyes shot open and she quickly turned off the water.

This made Michael stand straight up as if he was busted for stealing cookies like a little child.

"Look I know you're trying to deal with all the emotional changes, but just what'd you think you'd gain watching me shower?"

With one step he was inches away from her. Without taking his eyes away from her face, he reached for the nearby towel and wrapped it around her. With slow strokes, he began to dry her off. Not until he was done did he break the deafening silence. By this time he was standing behind her so they could see their reflection in the bathroom mirror.

"I've seen many women in my time, yet you pull me like none other," he said just above a whisper.

Swallowing hard, Xian just stared back at his reflection. Not knowing what to say or do; deciding to remain quiet and still. Seeing she was unsure of how to act he continued,

"Since we are to be together as more than we both initially thought, I wanted to take as much time as possible before knowing you physically; emotionally. Humans have such fierce levels of love and hate. I need to be sure you've accepted me before taking things further. No matter what, we have to fight together an enemy that will use any means to separate and defeat us. If being with me is something you can't be open to, then we should leave our relationship as is."

After taking a long deep breath she turned to face him. His eyes were in a constant flux, changing colors as she stared at him. Her heart began to race so fast the longer she stared, until she closed her eyes to try and slow it down. She focused on the cold tiles beneath her feet to stop from seeing his blue energy reaching for her.

"Do you want me Xian?" he said in a deep throaty tone.

Her mouth felt drier than before so all she could do was nod.

"Say what you mean. You have to say it out loud; bring it into this realm."

Xian swallowed hard trying to get the saliva going again in her mouth. A deep breath in and then she let her heart spill out in one brief statement,

"Yes I want you, from the first moment I saw you, there's been only you in my heart."

Michael let a smile creep across his face. Finally he let out the breath he was holding. Relief covered him knowing that she was committed to their cause and to him. He kissed her again on her forehead, wrapped the towel tighter around now dry body, placing her hands to hold it in place, as he left the bathroom. Xian just stared at the half closed door. *Alright weird confession moment and then he just leaves…did I miss something?* Realizing he wasn't coming back, she quickly dressed in a t-shirt and shorts. Her bedroom was empty so she walked cautiously out into the living room not sure if he'd left or not. She found Michael lying on the sofa, scanning the pages of the day's newspaper local section.

Not sure what to do, she just stood there waiting for him to say something. Without a word he placed the paper on the coffee table and reached his hand to her. Shyly taking it, he pulled her down to lay next to him as he scooted against the back as far as he could. Gently he pushed her damp curls away from her face so that the majority hung over the edge of the seat.

"Sleep beautiful one. I have no intention of taking our relationship further tonight. I just had to know you were with me in every way."

She looked up at him and smiled. It was all she could do not to reach up and kiss him. If he thought he was alone in reining back emotions, he was mistaken. The mere sight of him made her weak inside. It had been quite a while since she let herself feel for anyone. Not wanting to blow it, she opted to stroke the side of his face instead, and then she snuggled closer, giving in to the weight of her eyelids and the sweet slumber that beckoned to her.

CHAPTER 12

After Michael had put Xian through a long morning training session, they sat on some crates near the edge of her apartment's roof. The mornings sun was bright and its heat had started to warm the city. Refreshing themselves on a selection of fruit and citrus infused water, Michael decided it was time to tell her about Richard. When she had finished her last piece of melon, he cleared his throat and started.

He described the childhood Richard had endured and the moment Satan had tricked the vulnerable boy into his servitude. Xian just listened as she gazes over the cityscape, feeling sympathy for Richard for all he'd been through. She kept quiet until Michael recounted the string of events that had ultimately intertwined their fates.

"So he doesn't really have any gifts, just being used by Satan?" She asked now looking at Michael who turned to face her.

"No, none in the sense that you have, however he is powerful because of Satan's control over him. He's more of a puppet, no free will to speak of."

The rhythm of the now busy streets below entertained the void between them, broken when Xian then asked,

"So what exactly am I to do with him? If he's not really a fighter and has no powers, why is he such a threat?"

"His threat is that he's the physical hand that Satan is using to mark people for demonic possession. Satan has him teamed up with a woman named Jenny who also has been heavily influenced by Satan since a child. Basically, Satan plans to have them become his Adam and Eve in this era to bring into this realm a mass demonic army."

"Thus the marked people," Xian said nodding as the pieces started to fit in her mind. "Do I have what it takes to stop him? I know he has no powers, but being controlled by Satan I'm sure he has a few tricks, right?"

"You're right to assume he has some tricks but it's a bit more than that, and yes you have what it takes to stop him," Michael said as he motioned for her to follow him back to the center of the roof.

Without warning he let his true self-attack her. Without hesitation, she side stepped him and took a defensive stance. He charged again only, this time going for her legs trying to get her to loose balance so he could strike a killing blow to the head as she fell. Xian was light on her feet and did a sideways air cartwheel. Michael smiled as he admired her form. When she landed he was taken by surprise as she directed energy towards him, pushing him back a few inches. With his head slightly tilted to the side, he gave her a raised eyebrow look. She smirked in response.

They continued to fight for a few more minutes, with each attack he gave, she countered by mostly avoiding then striking back until he had her backed up against a sign pole. She wasn't fast enough to dodge him and they both knew it.

Ahh I really didn't pay enough attention to my surroundings on that last move, she thought begining to feel a little afraid. If Michael was a real threat she would be in serious trouble right now. Okay then, since I've nothing else to get me out of this mess, let's see how well I can channel this energy in me, she thought starting to pull all her reserves from deep inside. The wave of heat rushed through her so powerfully; it took some effort not to fall forward. When Michael was within two feet of her, the energy became a glowing shield of light with flames licking out at the edges. He stopped dead in his tracks; a loud roaring laugh burst from his lips.

"Yes, yes, yes. Now you yourself can see you're ready to take anything on."

Realizing he wasn't going to continue attacking, Xian relaxed and the shield slowly faded away. Feeling like she had a major sugar rush she giggled and began to pace, shaking her arms and trying to formulate a coherent sentence.

"Relax, just take deep breaths. You'll get used to it the more you use it," Michael calmly said as he reached

for her hands trying to help settle her nerves.

"It felt so strong, I mean I almost fell over," she gushed out looking wide-eyed up at him. His face wasn't making her feel any calmer, instead her emotions were raw and all she wanted to do was just jump into his arms, wrapping her body around his and kissing those lips she'd daydreamed of from day one.

Seeing the look change in her eye, he tightened his grip on her hands pushing against her forward advancement. She looked so innocent and sweet. He could feel the heat coming from her body as the chemical changes were still all out of whack. Her heart beat was still racing and if one of them didn't make a clear-headed decision within the next few seconds, they would be tearing at each other's clothes for certain. He wanted her, yes but not like this. She was precious and deserved the best and he planned to show her starting now.

Without another word, he pulled her behind him toward the door of the stairwell. Still unsettled by the flood of emotions coursing through her body, Xian complied silently glad he was taking control as she was in no shape to make any decisions. Once they were in her apartment, he told her to change and wait for him; he'd be back within an hour. Glad for a cold shower, Xian waved and nodded as she went towards her bathroom. Once he'd made sure the apartment was being guarded by the Watcher Angels nearby, Michael headed to Marcus' shop.

Marcus was busy going through a small book that looked to be written on animal hide. Knowing it was Michael before he entered the store, Marcus casually said hello without glancing away from the page that had held his attention for some hours now.

"I need a ring and you to perform the ceremony."

Slowly looking up from his book, Marcus saw Michael standing there face wearing a serious stare. Smirking he nodded and motioned with his head for Michael to follow him over to a shelf further into the store. Reaching behind a set of books, Marcus pulled out a stone, which looked more like a broken piece of a wall. As Michael looked on a bit confused, Marcus squeezed and pieces crumbled away. What remained in his hand was a ring, itself made of a molten red-orange gem that wasn't that bright nor shiny.

Michael fingered it once Marcus handed it over. Holding it up to see how the light would reflect off of it, he looked at Marcus with a questioning expression.

"Not much to look at now but, once she wears it, the gem will reflect her energy and trust me, it's a real show stopper."

"Fine, I still need you to come and perform the ceremony. It's time and the local resistance is gaining momentum again. The head of the snake needs to be dealt with."

"About time you made a move. I know you want her to be ready but, holding out on her emotional needs was painful even for me to watch."

"For you to watch; you've met her only once. How do you know anything about her emotional needs?" Michael said with a slight chuckle.

"I may not be the tallest man in the room, but I saw how she looked at you and did we forget the impromptu visit you gave me not so long ago?"

Laughing at it all they both made their way back to Xian's apartment. Michael hoped she was dressed and waiting, though he suspected she might not be especially after this morning's exercise, knowing her she was mostly likely having a good long shower.

The cold water did the trick of helping calm Xian's nerves; well for the most part. Most of her thoughts now focused on this Richard guy. She still wasn't sure what the plan was for taking him out. *Am I supposed to actually take him out since he isn't really possessed but being used by Satan like a puppet?* She wondered as she fastened the last button on her blouse. Just as she finished with the button, the apartment front door opened and the sound of multiple footsteps made her become defensive. Reaching for her sword she turned to investigate only to walk into the hard chest of Michael. Her shoulders dropped in relief.

"We need to talk," he said closing the room door behind him then motioning for her to have a seat on the bed.

Running his right hand through his hair, he had planned to give a long explanation to her on the way over but now in the moment, his mind was blank. It just had to be these roller-coaster emotions he was plagued with. Seeing he was a bit uneasy, Xian reached out her hand and touched his side, stopping him in suddenly. She was staring up at him with such tenderness all he could do was kneel down next to her. Gently he touched her face and let out a long sigh. He held her gaze for a few seconds more then slowly said,

"I've explained how our lives have become connected and I know it's been a challenge for both of us to keep focused on training and stuff. You are so precious for lots of reasons, but in particular you've given me new purpose. My life was complete before you because there was no void to fill. Now, things have changed." He pulled the ring from his pocket and held it up for her to see.

Xian gasped when she saw it. Slowly the color became brighter as it fed off her energy. She peeled her eyes away from it and stared into light blue pools. Michael's true form was coming forward in his body and then she barely heard him ask,

"Xian, will you marry me?"

She didn't even realize tears had started to fill her eyes until she felt the first one roll down her right cheek. Michael gently brushed it away just as she finally spoke the first word,

"Yes, yes I will marry you Michael," by this time the other tears had began a free fall as he slipped the ring onto her ring finger. Pull her chin up towards him he kissed her on the forehead, and then he rose to his feet.

"Come, let's get this made official."

Still staring at her ring while following him into the living room, Xian didn't see Marcus sitting on the sofa. He cleared his throat making her head snap up to find him now standing with the biggest, almost scariest grin she'd ever seen.

"Congratulations my dear, I was wondering when this big brute would get the nerve and pop the question. Okay let's just stand right over here out of view of the window; never know who may be watching."

Looking a bit confused, Michael explained to Xian that Marcus was going to officiate in their marriage. He promised they could have the big fussy wedding later if she wanted. His intention was to have them married as soon as possible, so he could give her one last piece of weaponry. Still not fully understanding just what he was getting at, she just nodded and stood next to him, waiting for Marcus to begin.

CHAPTER 13

That night when they were alone again, Xian thought of how much life had changed for her in the past few months. She was the happiest she'd ever been in as long as she could remember and her skin tingled with anticipation of what was to come next. Here she now was married, driving along the highway to who knows where with the man who only existed in her dreams. In her heart she said a thankful prayer and turned to him, taking a lock of his hair to twirl in her fingers. All the fighting and threats that were around them in the city couldn't dampen her mood; she was on top of the world.

Michael pulled her car into a marina's parking lot. She looked and saw there was hardly anyone around. Following his lead, she walked along the sidewalk until they stopped in front of a gorgeous yacht. As if out of nowhere, a man came from inside it and offered to take their bags. Once inside, they were greeted by a woman dressed in white shorts and a dark blue t-shirt. She directed them to their sleeping quarters and advised that dinner would be served in fifteen minutes. By the time Xian got to look around the sleeping area, they felt the ship moving out to sea.

"Ah what is all this? I'm not complaining just a bit surprised with all that's happened today. How long have you been planning this?"

"The yacht is always at our disposal and I planned this right after our morning practice."

"Will we be spending all our time on this?" she asked running her hand along the high gloss wooden finish of the dressing table.

"No, we're using it as a means to get to the island. I thought it would be more romantic than me flying us there with luggage," he chuckled.

Nodding in agreement, she smiled at him while rubbing her growling stomach. Taking her cue, he led them up to the dining area where the table was beautifully spread with several dishes, all she noted similar to the ones they five stared at their favorite dinner. Shaking her head and smiling she took her seat, eager to sample a little of everything. The water was calm so their ride was pretty smooth. Xian was grateful for this as she wasn't sure if she really had sea legs and tonight was not the one she wanted to test that theory with.

Desert was a small six-inch cake that had a bride and groom standing on top. She touched his arm smiling to show him how much she appreciated all the little things he'd thought of in such a short time. Holding the shining silver knife, they cut the cake and fed each other a mouthful. Buttery icing covered their lips as they both smiled agreeing how delicious it was. Michael truly loved her non-pretentious attitude when it came to eating in front of him. She could hold her own. When they were both stuffed, they decided to go out onto the deck and enjoy the beautiful night. The air wasn't too cool and the moon cast a bright glow on the water. Just ahead, Xian could make out the island it looked different from this angle since the first time she saw it was from above, holding onto Michael for dear life.

They docked and as soon as they both had taken just a few steps, lights flicked on then cheers erupted. Michael had to hold Xian's shoulders as she almost fell backward towards the docks edge. Letting out a scream and holding her chest she stared back into the smiling faces of angels that lived on the island. Her guard had been down since she knew that where they were headed was a safe haven. Once the initial shock had worn off and Michael saw she was alright, he let go of her and gently pulled her hand to follow him up to the main building.

Cheers and well wishes continued until they reached the main building where Xian was introduced to new faces that she hadn't met the last time she was there.

Thankful for there not being a long drawn out meet and greet, they followed a lighted path away from the dock and main building. They passed several small bungalows then what looked like a garden. The aroma of mixed flowers filled the air and Xian inhaled deeply as they walked. The path then turned right, ending in front of a small bungalow. The lights inside were already on and once inside, Xian saw that the back wall was nothing but floor to ceiling sliding doors, all of which were open letting in the light sea breeze.

Her face lit up in appreciation as she walked around inspecting all the rooms. There was a kitchen with bar counter top just off the living area and next to it was a large bedroom with a pretty spacious bathroom attached. Emerging from the bedroom she found Michael standing next to one of the openings leading out onto the beach just a few feet away; shirtless. Her breath caught in her throat as she looked at his back. Even from this angle she was powerless when it came to him; his hold on her was strong and for once she never wanted to resist. Knowing he was being watched by her, Michael held out his hand beckoning her to him. Happy to be by his side she approached, only to be picked up in his arms and carried off to the bedroom. Xian let her head rest against his shoulder. She took deep breaths to try and settle her racing pulse. The moment she had thought would only be a dream was here. Nothing mattered in this moment. She closed her mind's door of the outside world, wanting to live only in this time, engraving the memories to her heart.

Richard knew he'd have to make a decision sooner than later. His hectic schedule of his day job and the tiring things Buddy had him doing every night was more than his body could handle. He'd started to lose some weight and the color was almost drained from his face. To ward off any questioning looks at work, he'd resorted to using a tinted moisturizer. Shaking his head at the turn his life had taken recently, he pulled a stack of folders towards him on his desk and tried to prioritize the load he'd be given. By lunch time he knew there was no choice, something had to give. If he looked like he'd worked himself to death, Buddy wouldn't get his way and maybe, just maybe, he'd be off the hook. He could have some type of normal life back; maybe. *I'm just going to lay it all on the line for him, he'll have to see reason,* he thought as he slurped down the last of his soda while making his way back to his desk from the break room.

Just then his cell phone rang. He didn't recognize the number but decided to answer it instead of letting it go to voicemail. The moment he heard the voice his heart skipped; it was Jenny.

"Hey Sport, how you doing?"

"Hey, oh ah I'm doing okay, how about you?" he replied running his left hand through his hair. He tried to use as cheerful a voice as possible, which wasn't really hard considering who he was talking to. But Jenny picked up on the slight strain that came through.

"Are you getting any sleep? I know I've been getting only a few good hours a night but I have a feeling you're being kept occupied more than I am after dark."

The pause was longer than Richard had wanted it to be after she spoke. He was trying really hard to think of something cool to say, but his brain was just too tired. Instead he let out a long sigh.

"Look if you're tired why not go home early and try to get some rest?" she said as sympathetic as she could.

"Yeah, maybe that would help some, but I have a lot to get done this week and the department is already short staffed due to others out on vacation," he let out another sigh before continuing, "I think I'll be okay after a late afternoon cup of espresso."

By this time he was at his desk scanning the files he had prioritized. Deciding he'd wing it this week to see how things went with Buddy and if worst case scenario ended up as the only option, he'd have to quit his job before this draining lifestyle had him end up cold on a steel slab in the morgue. Sensing it wasn't the best time to bring up her favors for the project folder in her hands, Jenny decided to let him be for now. After exchanging their goodbyes, Richard dug into the workload and tried to push all thoughts of Buddy and his agenda out of his head. He thought briefly how his work helped him not to think of much else. It allowed his mind to focus only on what was in front of him. However, all peace ended with Buddy. It was so easy to get tangled up with him. *I was such a weak punk. Why didn't I see that I was trading one misery for another back then? There's just got to be a way to be free; I must be free of him.* He screamed silently to himself.

    From the time he returned to his desk from lunch to six thirty went by in a blur. Richard was so tuned out to the others around him he hadn't noticed when they began to trickle out the office one by one. The honking of car horns from the evening traffic made him look up to notice the sun was beginning to set, leaving behind a streak of yellow and orange across the glass windows on the far wall. His shoulders were stiff and when he twisted his neck and shrugged them, loud popping sounds surrounded him. He'd had enough for one day. Regardless, tonight he planned to sleep. No gatherings for him and Buddy had better pester someone else. One way or another he was going to have peace.

With great relief, Richard managed to get home without any interruptions. No voice whispered in his head, and thankfully, no one was walking alongside him with messages or directions to some new location around town. The hot shower worked out the last of his stiff shoulders and after heating up the frozen dinner, he sat down his small table to eat. Looking around his small apartment, the drabness of it seemed to hit him for the first time. Plain grayish walls with dark draped windows made it look almost like a dungeon. The dim lighting from the side lamp didn't help much, only casting shadows on the long dark brown sofa on the opposite wall under the window.

"First thing this weekend Richie Boy is getting some brighter paint for these walls. A set of sheer curtains and brighter lighting also are on the list," he said out loud to himself, mimicking the voice of his favorite local sportscaster. No matter how bad a team was losing, he always found a bright side and put on his motivational speaker like tone when he spoke into the headset. Nodding in agreement, he envisioned some brighter shades on the wall, maybe something a soft yellow, a new rug with contrasting tones to liven up the floor too. Smiling now, he felt kind of normal. Like a new person without the cares of the world on his back. Enjoying the momentum, he cleared his dishes and headed to bed. Deciding to check out some sports on cable TV he got comfortable in bed as he tuned in just in time to catch the start of some college basketball.

    It wasn't long before his eyes became heavy, not wanting to be in a silent room, he turned down the volume a little lower, flicked off the light and removed the extra pillows from under his head. Before the next commercial came on, he was out cold. Sweet sleep took him off to a place of emptiness. His mind for a long time had nothing led his ears. Then the sound of his neighbor's door closing broke him from his daze. Stretching his arms and legs, he slowly opened his eyes, trying to figure out how long he'd been asleep. A few rays of morning light mixed with the picture on the TV screen, causing him to squint so he could focus on the picture. The basketball game was long over and highlights from the prior day's sporting events were being flashed across the screen.

    The alarm sounded, making him look over at his clock to see it was going on 7:00 a.m. Rubbing his eyes, and then staring at the ceiling he realized he'd slept straight through the night. Sweet uninterrupted sleep had finally been his. Smiling to himself, he mentally picked out what he'd wear to work as he headed to the shower. While getting dressed and looking in his dresser mirror, hope started to spark in his heart. Hope that maybe he really could be free of Buddy. It had been over twenty-four hours since he'd heard his voice and with every second that the time grew, his hope sparked a bit brighter. His cell phone rang and seeing it was Jenny, he almost sang his greeting into the phone.

"Well someone is feeling better this morning. I'm really glad to see you got some rest last night," she said before laughing a little at his high pitched voice.

"Yes, someone did get quite rested last night, thank you. How did you sleep last night?"

"Ah well some of us had deadlines to meet and other things going on, but at least one of us can maybe squeeze in a favor for the other today. I mean since they're so rested and all?" she teased with a little pleading tone at the end.

"Oh yeah, a little favor huh? I should have known this was no sweet-morning-promises call," he chuckled back at her.

Agreeing to meet up for coffee first thing at work, they ended the call and Richard grabbed his jacket, double checking his pant pocket for his wallet before snatching his keys from the kitchen counter and stepping out of his apartment. A few other neighbors were also locking up then making their way towards the elevator. Not wanting to risk being cornered by any of Buddy's people so early, he opted for the stairwell closer to him. Most tenants took the elevator, so he knew he'd pretty much be alone taking the three flights down. Anything was better than the alternative to him, besides he could scurry down the stairs faster than the elevator that undoubtedly would be stopping or held up by the swarm about to leave for work.

  Sure enough he emerged into the lobby before the crowded box opened onto the main floor. Within less than twenty seconds, he was out on the sidewalk taking in a full breath of fresh morning air. Everything felt new to him the scent of the breakfast cart near the corner filled his nose, making his stomach rumble. Quickly he got there before his neighbors, who were now speed walking his way. He picked up two sandwiches then crossed the street towards his parked car in the garage just ahead. He planned to give one of them to Jenny and maybe see if she'd hang out later. The thought of her lit a small fire in his groin. Trying not to let his thoughts get too carried away, he turned on the radio and let the morning talk show hosts fill his head with meaningless chatter.

  When he got to work Jenny was already in the break room. She was standing near the coffee pots fixing a cup when he gently placed her sandwich next to her.

"Good morning beautiful," he almost whispered in her right ear.

His warm breath made her shiver slightly as her body tensed, then relaxed once she figured it was him. Acting as if he had no effect on her, she tried to casually continue mixing the creamer into her cup.

"Good morning to you to bearer of food," turning now to face him she smiled slightly bowing.

The both laughed and headed to one of the empty tables. Almost inhaling their breakfast, they went over the favor Jenny wanted for the project she was under the gun to finish by the end of the day. Seeing it would only take him about an hour to help her, Richard twisted his mouth as he scanned the portfolio before saying,

"Well since I will be pushing aside my workload to help you out this crisis, you will owe me one."

"Sure, name it. I just can't afford to be late with this today," she replied relieved he'd come to her rescue.

"Dinner at my place, or your place if you'd be more comfortable," he interjected, not wanting to scare her off.

With a raised eyebrow she looked at him then back at her almost empty coffee cup. A small smile curved at her lips as she pretended to ponder his proposal. Knowing full well she was game for almost anything to get what she wanted, she slowly let out a breath and pretended like she was only going along with his request to pay back the favor she desperately needed.

"Sure, why not. Let's say my place and as a thank you I'll provide dinner; take out of course since I won't have much time to cook after handing off this presentation."

"Of course, take out will be just fine. Let's say around 7:30 p.m. then?" he said slowly eyeing her as much as the obscuring table would allow. He didn't miss it when she took a hard swallow and the rising of her chest when she nodded in agreement to the time. The lingering scent of her body enveloped him as he followed her to the door. The sway of her hips in her skirt dared to rekindle the fire he had worked so hard to put out earlier.

It's going to be a challenging day to keep focused, he thought as they parted ways just beyond the break room door.

The rest of the day went by fairly quickly. Richard was able to squeeze in Jenny's request and still turn over two more of his projects to his boss for review. A good night's sleep surely made a huge difference. He was feeling surer of his self than he'd felt in a while, he stretch back in his chair as far as it would recline; a big smile plastered on his face and eyes closed. Enjoying this newfound freedom, he sat back up and rotated his neck before picking up the next folder from the pile on his desk. It wasn't long before the office started to get noisy with the usually departing speeches and the rustling of keys. Checking the time on his computer screen, Richard saw he had just over an hour before he was to meet up with Jenny. She'd texted her address along with detailed directions to make sure he didn't get lost. Smiling as he read it, Richard made his way to his car. He'd have just enough time to go home for a quick change. A long forgotten tune came to mind and instinctively his lips parted to whistle along. The spark of hope continued to grow.

CHAPTER 14

Jenny was fussing over what to wear, pacing along the side of her bed staring at the clothes spread out on it. She wanted something that seemed cute but not too casual, sexy but not too obvious. Glancing at the bedside clock the red neon numbers let her know she had thirty more minutes before Richard was to arrive. Deciding to go with the cap sleeved dress; she reached into the closet for a pair of heeled slippers. Her hair was almost dry from the quick shampooing and instead of perfume; she opted for the scented body lotion she'd received as a Christmas gift in the office gift exchange at work. The combination of scents from her hair and lotion, made her smell like a summer's mixed floral bouquet. Regardless what Richard thought tonight was going to be about, she had one goal; per instructions, get his mind back in the game.

Not soon after she had set the table with the takeout she'd picked up on the way home, did her doorbell ring. Letting out a deep breath and checking her reflection in the oval mirror near the door, she smiled and let Richard inside.

He smiled when seeing her, passed the small bunch of white roses and walked past her into the small foyer space. Inhaling the rose's sweet aroma, she thanked him and led them towards the dining table. Holding up the bottle of wine, she motioned towards the kitchen where she filled a vase with water for the roses and pointed to a side drawer for him to get the bottle opener.

Each was caught up in their own thoughts, she thinking how different he looked the past few days and how suddenly handsome he seemed. His cologne was just strong enough to make her subconsciously follow him with her nose. Taking a side glance at him as she finished arranging the roses, she got a good look at his profile, scanning down to his toned lower body. It had been almost two years since she'd been with a man, mostly of her own doing. Being this close now to one, especially one she had so much in common with, made her rethink about being on lockdown.

Richard managed to open the wine bottle without much fuss and took two glasses from the rack hanging under the cabinets. He walked back to the table, setting them next to empty plates. He looked up just in time to see Jenny approaching with the rose filled vase. As she leaned to place it in the center of the table, he caught a peek of her breast. Her skin looked dewy and begging to be touched. He forced himself to look away and focus more on the spread of food. Jenny had picked up some roasted chicken and battered shrimp, complemented with sides of salad, mixed vegetables, baked potato and slices of apple pie. Licking his lips he held her chair for her, accidently brushing her shoulders with his fingers when she leaned back into the seat.

Dinner was not much on talk, except the occasional compliment on the taste of the food. Jenny told him of the restaurant she got it from and suggested maybe they could eat there another time. Smiling at the prospect of spending more time with her alone, Richard agreed. Seeing that she needed to make better progress with her plan, Jenny poked him with a question while enjoying her slice of apple pie,

"How have you been able to balance your night responsibility lately, you seem to be different somehow?"

"Ah well actually, there hasn't been anything to balance. I mean for a while I was running on fumes, but now nothing. I go through my day without any voices and slept like a rock the other night."

He's actually happy, she thought; *look at him feeling all free and what not. Yeah this one definitely thinks he's getting away that easily. Hmm, don't worry Richard; I'm going to make sure you stay on track. Besides, we are to be a team, the Adam and Eve of this new world order;*

and I intend to have my crown one way or another. Smiling back at him she said,

"Well I'm happy you've gotten some free time and rest. You look ready to take on the world. Are you done eating?"

"Oh yes thanks, the food again was delicious. It really tasted homemade. The company has been exceptional as well so far," he said giving her a sly look, purposely letting his gaze hold hers until she shifted from discomfort. The thin fabric of her dress clung just right and he noticed her nipples hardening under his stare.

Deciding she needed to take back control of the evening, Jenny got up and began to clear the table. On cue, Richard assisted following her into the kitchen and gathering up the scraps along with takeout containers, filling up the trash can which was now unable to close due to the amount of garbage. Without hesitation, he secured the trash bag and holding it up looked at her questioningly as to where to dump it. Understanding his look, she directed him down the hall to the first steel door. Silently he left the apartment as she continued to clean up the kitchen.

When he got back, she was now sitting on the balcony, both of their wine glasses had been placed on the small table between matching lounge chairs. Her hair was now gently moving in the night's air. It was another cool evening in the city, probably the last before the temperature climbed again. He took his seat in the vacant chair and drank from his glass.

"I love to come out here and look at the stars," she said still gazing up into the clear sky.

"It really is a nice spot and you've got a great view of the city skyline."

"This was the selling point for me on this apartment. That and the fact that the walls are pretty much sound proof."

Almost choking on the last statement, Richard placed his glass back on the table. She was now staring at him seductively, running her finger around the rim of the wine glass. A low humming came from it, almost pulling him to her. She could see the desire creeping up fast in his eyes, knowing she had him just where she wanted, Jenny asked,

"So how do you think we should proceed with Buddy's plans? I've been trying to figure out how to make the most of the few hours a day we have free outside work?"

Richard hesitated before speaking. His desire cut and the sickening feeling started to return to his stomach at the thought of Buddy controlling him again. Not wanting to give away his thoughts, he held her gaze and softly replied,

"One thing I know about Buddy, is he takes care of the small things. Our lack of time for instance, he knows we can't keep this pace for much longer, so he'll give us no other choice really but to quit working."

"I can't do that, I mean I have bills to pay, stuff to buy," she said with a bit of panic in her voice.

"Yeah I know what you mean, but he does own almost all the city, so I'm sure we'll be taken care of."

Seeing Richard didn't look fazed by these facts, Jenny sat up and motioned for him to work out a kink in her neck. The stress of the past few weeks was getting to her; she also wasn't getting the amount of sleep she wished for. Without missing a beat, Richard was standing behind her gently massaging her shoulders and neck. He found the knot and began to work at it. Just as he'd imagined, her skin did feel good. The slight moisture on it acted as a massaging lotion; the moment she let her head fall forward exposing the nape of her neck made him loose it. Enough of this coy game, she wanted him just a bad and either way sooner or later they'd be together, why not tonight? Her words though, faintly echoed in his ears about working for Buddy. *Didn't she want out too? I mean why would she want to stay hooked up to him? What is her real deal?* He thought before the heat in his groin took over and his lips now trailed the length of her neck as his hand slipped under the opening of her dress, caressing her rock hard nipples.

CHAPTER 15

It had been a long glorious week of no Buddy for Richard. He was a new man. Work was getting churned out and almost every night he had Jenny wrapped up in his arms. He practically lived at her place over the past few days. She had quickly consumed him; she was all he thought of; wanted. Just as Buddy had called it, he knew Richard longed for a loving connection and who better than Jenny. They shared a strong understanding of the real world around them and soon, they would play out his ultimate plan for their pathetic lives. Lust was a powerful drug and after another few days of passion, Richard would be willing to do whatever he wanted him to.

Satan smiled as he sat on his throne looking down at Richard as he took Jenny throughout the night, not knowing with each touch he was falling deeper into Satan's will. That week was the beginning of the end for both of them. Early Friday morning he had them resign their jobs and move into one of his compounds. When they got there later in the day, all their belongings were neatly filling the three bedroom penthouse. The view was way better than the one at Jenny's old apartment since it had a wraparound balcony on three sides of the glass windowed walls. There was a maid fully uniformed waiting to show them around, advising a light snack had been prepared for them out on the main terrace.

Like playing out a role in some movie, Jenny swirled around the terrace giggling. She'd made it; finally made it. No more begging and hustling to get her piece of life. She was now queen of this city, whether it knew or not. Looking over at Richard who just stared around frowning, she pulled him further out onto the terrace.

"What's up with the sour face? Isn't this place amazing? I mean we don't have to work and just like you said, we're being taken care of."

"Yeah we're being taken care of, but at what price?"

"Come on Richard you know it's bigger than both of us. Just go with it. There's nothing you can do to stop him anyways," she said before rubbing her hands along the front of him pants, "just enjoy the ride Baby."

Pushing her hand away he stepped to the edge with both hands on the railing. It finally made sense to him. The past few weeks of peace without Buddy was replaced by the conniving actions of his other tool; Jenny. Slowly shaking his head at how easily he fell for her charms, he twisted his lips and nodded. *Fine then, if they both want to play then let's play. I've nothing to lose anyways and can't see my way out of this mess. Access to sweet ass every night, lavish living, and a city at my feet; who wouldn't want this?* He thought before turning to face her. She was now standing behind him trying to read his thoughts. He just smiled, pulled her close then he devoured her mouth before leading them over to table spread of snacks prepared for them.

"Yeah you're right Baby, let's enjoy the ride," he said in his most convincing voice, but deep inside he struggled to keep the flame of hope lit.

The sounds of gently crashing waves along the nearby shore, stirred Xian awake. With eyes still closed she pointed her toes under the thin sheet and was about to stretch her arms wide when she hit something hard. With a jolt her eyes flew open to take in the well-sculpted chest of Michael. He lied there as if asleep. She felt he was pretending, but wasn't sure since he had been acting more human since returning from Heaven. Not wanting to give away the fact that she was awake, she just stared at his body. *So it wasn't a dream. Yesterday and last night really happened,* she thought to herself.

Her mind played out the events from the moment Michael placed her on the bed. He kissed her and then everything felt like it was happening in slow motion. The sensations she felt from his touch made her light headed and by the time they joined, she was on the edge ready to fall over. To say it was worth the wait didn't do it justice. A sudden smile was on her face as Michael slowly pulled her chin up to look at him. She knew she was busted, as her eyes and body now betrayed her. *Who cares? He's all mine now and I will not pretend I don't want him. God how I want him*, she thought as her eyes stared back into light blue pools.

His true form was looking back at her and with each passing second, she melted. Deciding to be bold, she reached up and pulled him downwards to close the gap between them. Willingly he obliged and soon they were exploring each other again. This time Xian kept repeating to herself that it was no dream. They continued to enjoy each other for a long time, only the thunderous growling of her stomach made them break and head to the kitchen. A brunch spread was waiting for them and Xian was too grateful for it to care what was or wasn't there. She sampled everything a mouthfull at a time as she piled her plate. Noticing that Michael was observing her delight, she paused and said,

"Wow, barely married a day and I've already lost my manners. Sit; let me fix you a plate. A little of everything, right or what don't you feel like eating?"

With a grin he pulled up a chair and told her he'd take some of everything. The day was bright and starting to get warm by the time they finished the spread. Stuffed they decided to relax on the patio, in no hurry to do anything else. Xian enjoyed the warmth of the sun beating down on her barely clothed body. Michael still shirtless watched her for a few moments then let his eye drift out towards the horizon. Try as he could, he was unable to enjoy the moment for long. His thoughts were back in Miami and all the damage they'd have to face once returning. *I know this is supposed to be our break from it all, but can we really afford the time away?* He thought before Xian's hand was tugging at his pants waistband.

"Hey where'd you go so fast, huh? I know you didn't mentally leave me here all alone," she teased.

Shaking his head, not wanting to upset her, he smiled and stood up pulling her behind him. They ended up in the bathroom where Michael proceeded to prepare a bath for them. Thinking it was just for her, Xian started to undress, looking at him wide-eyed when seeing he wasn't leaving the room.

"So we have consummated our marriage more than once yet you don't want me in the bathroom with you while taking a bath?" he asked now with folded arms across his chest and tilted head.

"My bad, I just thought you were being even sweeter and preparing me a nice bath to relax my slightly aching muscles," she replied with an exaggerated pout.

"I am being sweeter. I'm going to share this bath with you and take care of those slightly aching muscles," he said holding up his hands to make imaginary quotation marks.

They both burst out laughing while the huge tub continued to fill with warm bubbly water. Once inside, Michael motioned for her to sit with her back to him. Reaching for scented oils in a nearby basket, he rubbed the oil in his hands until it was quite warm. As soon as he touched her shoulders, Xian let out a low moan. His hands did a slow dance across her shoulders then up the sides of her neck. Taking his time, Michael continued to knead away until she had let all of her weight rest on his hands. Slowly he let her fall backward until she was lying on his chest. The warmth generated by his massage and that of the water had her almost asleep. Feeling her like this aroused him, which in turn pulled her back from the tip of a nap.

Smiling with her eyes still closed she rubbed his legs on either side of her and then initiated another round of bonding with the specimen she now called husband. Needless to say the water was cold when they finally got out. The rest of the afternoon was passed by more eating food that seemed to appear whenever her stomach started growling and exploring their side of the island. Occasionally they explored each other under the palm trees but Xian stopped Michael whenever things were getting too heated. Laughing at her need for privacy, he decided not to press the issue but reminded her that the walls of the bungalow didn't really shield them from those on the island since they could see through them. The look on her face after his words sank in made her complexion go ghostly pale. He couldn't hold in the roaring laugh and pulled her close, burying her head in his chest as if to hide her from possible onlookers; which he knew there were none.

    The remaining days they spent there were filled with private swimming, love making and almost any type of food she could want or imagine. She finally asked Michael how the food was suddenly appearing and he smiled as he explained they pretty much had her feeding schedule down to a science. They as in meaning the other angels on the island; who many had also been watching over her before Michael had been given the task of training her.

    "You mean they know me? They've watched me all this time?"

    "Yes. Many have been assigned to you since the day you were conceived. Your life has always had a significant part in The Fathers plan. I feel so honored to be given the chance to be more than you trainer," he said as he stopped walking along the shore, turning them both to watch the sun setting, "there are so many people out there that need us to complete our mission."

Turning his head slightly to look at her, he took a deep breath then while still watching for her reaction he said,

"Are you ready to go back?"

"Yes," her body never tensed when she spoke the word, which made him glad.

"Fine, we will leave in three days but until then my sweet," he said picking her up in his arms, "I will take in all of you while sharing all that I can of myself. This is our time and nothing's going to interfere with it."

She wrapped her arms around his neck, nuzzling it on the right side. His scent overwhelmed her senses and without thought she began a trail of kisses from his neck to his lips. After a few seconds he broke away, throwing her over his shoulder as he made a dash for the bungalow in non-human speed. He only had three more days of relevant peace with her, all of which he planned to enjoy immensely.

Feeling the need for some testing of skills, Michael suggested they go for a late night swim. The evening was not that hot and the sky was filled with a huge full moon. Without hesitation Xian agreed and soon they were playing in the warm sea. Just as she sprang up from under the water, Michael threw a punch at her head; blocked. Even Xian was smiling once their eyes met at her effortless reaction.

"Glad to see you're still sharp and alert. Good; very good."

"You're always telling me to be aware of what's going on around me. Did you think just because we're on our honeymoon I'd get lazy; become an easy target?"

"Hmmm, not really. I'm happy to see that you didn't. Less retraining for me when we get back to the mainland, also it means you're ready to amplify your skill level," he said while backing up from her until he was about ten feet away.

She steadied herself against the waves making their way to the shore, never taking her eyes off his. Xian knew from his now blank expression, a new lesson was about to begin. *Bring it,!* she said with her widening eyes and tilted head. Then just like that she felt an intense heat, almost scalding. Interestingly though the water itself never changed temperature, just her skin.

"That was just a low-level feel I gave you. Imagine what it could do in a fight at full strength," he said not leaving his spot, "you good?"

"Yeah, I'm good. So how do I get to full strength?"

"I like yourr eagerness, but this will take not only visualizing the heat but pulling it from your mind out your body and onto the target. A bit different from your other talent that flows out from your spirit; this requires focusing on a target while still being aware of everything around you. Losing the balance will open you up for attacks; creating a weak spot."

"Alright, so how do I not create a weak spot exactly?"

"Let's start by you imagining a burning flame, one that is roaring, growing in size and heat."

After a few minutes of concentrating on what Michael described she nodded that she had the image in her mind.

"Good. Now let the flame travel from your head out your body towards me. Keep the image in tack, don't let it break apart."

She focused hard, pushing the image out as he directed but only managed to get it halfway between them.

"It's okay, you did well but next time, don't look at the image once its traveling focus on the target instead. You need to switch from pulling it out to pushing it towards your mark."

Taking a deep breath and thinking over the instructions Michael had given her, Xian creates the image again. This time the flames were bigger and she swore she even felt some of the heat on her skin. Pushing it across the water she felt more confident and did as suggested, switching from pushing to pulling when the flames were half way from the mark; Michael. She stared at his chest now mostly out the water, not wanting to be distracted by his eyes. With the flames almost a foot away from him, she sensed something coming fast towards her right side. Not wanting to miss her mark again she pushed it harder while bracing herself for the approaching attack. Just as the flames spread over his chest, she turned to block a downward swing of an arm. Her block didn't stop the attacker completely as she turned her body to avoid a backhand quickly aiming for the other side of her face.

"Stop," Michael shouted.

Xian stood readying herself in case another blow was headed her way. Seeing her attacker now backing away she slowly relaxed her stance. It was an angel she didn't remember seeing upon arriving. Realizing she wasn't in any real danger, Xian turned back to face Michael who hadn't moved from his spot.

"You are a quick learner for sure. That will make this something you will master in no time. I want you to remember it is important to balance what you see physically and what you see with your spirit. When you have mastered this skill, you will not need to turn around to fight off an attacker. You'll be able to consume your target with flames while defeating attackers despite the direction they come from. Got it?"

"Got it," she said repositioning herself to face him.

"Again," he shouted.

They repeated the drill several times. With each one Xian got better. Her confidence level rose and Michael began to feel some real heat from the flames she covered him with. The practice runs had now moved up onto the beach. Shadows cast by the nearby palms added to the challenge of her balancing her movements. It was on the last try she found her sweet spot. With a slight smirk she steadied herself for the next try. Michael caught it and knew things were about to get interesting. By this time they had an audience just a few feet behind the dense brush near each side of the bungalow. Xian didn't bother to pay them any attention knowing they weren't a threat. Michael's assistant attacker however, was something else entirely. They hadn't spoken at all but their fighting skills were not to be taken lightly.

Before the sound of his command to start faded on the evening breeze, Xian had already begun to push the image out of her mind towards Michael. As the flames hurled quickly towards him, she estimated they would reach their intended target in another three seconds. Xian stared past the flame and Michael letting her spirit show her the area around where she stood. Seeing the angel coming up fast dead center towards her back, she waited until she could sidestep to the left then follow through with a forward strike of her own. With two moves she had immobilized the attacker, while intensifying the flames that had covered just about all of Michael's body.

He was pleased to feel that the heat level had risen considerably; she was almost there. Deciding to push her just a bit harder to get her where she needed to be, he signaled for two more angels to assist in the practice session. He saw the seriousness in Xian's eyes and told them to not hold back. *Okay Sword of Vengeance, give me all you got or get the beat down of the week*, he thought staring just as intently back at her.

As he hoped, she laid it all on the line, nothing was held back. She was able to consume him completely this time with such an intense heat; it required him to dig deep into himself to cool his skin. A few strands of hair did singe though. She also made quick on taking care of the three angels that attacked one after the other. *I see you handle things better under pressure my dear; good to know*, he thought before he yelled,

"You can all come out now."

Slowly those that were spectating from the brush came onto the sand. They smiled and clapped in approval of what they'd just seen Xian do. The congratulations turned into an impromptu beach party of sorts. As if on cue, food was being passed to Xian along with a large bottle of water, which she almost drank in one shot. Laughing at his forever hungry wife, Michael smiled as he got closer to her.

"I'm so proud of you," he whispered in her ear before grabbing something to eat and drink for himself.

The party lasted for quite some time. Xian had made herself comfortable on a sand mound near a small bond fire. The flames mixed with the soothing sound of the sea coaxed her heavy eyelids to close. Deciding to let her rest there for a while, Michael continued to mingle with the others and talk about events they were involved in around the area. He learned that nearly every large city was being overrun by one of Satan's generals. Each taking over large populations and manipulating many of the locally prominent people, all who played some role or another in the cities take over by evil. After another hour of talking with them, Michael excused himself, picked up Xian who was fast asleep and made his way inside their bungalow.

She was still groggy when he managed to get them both into the shower. The hot water must have felt good to her as she moaned and let her weight rest on him while he lathered her up. Like a child she did the minimum while he cleaned her. Once done he wrapped her in a towel and put her under the covers on the bed. Returning to the bathroom, he let the cold shower water help ease the little lasting effects of her flames. He smiled as he nodded thinking back over her progression this evening. With a little more practice, she would be a real force to deal with. He made a mental note to have her hunt the minute they landed in Miami. *The more she fights the faster and stronger she'll become and from what the others told me, the war is getting uglier by the day*, he thought, *man she got me good with that last one though.*

CHAPTER 16

The day came quickly for them to leave. Xian had really enjoyed her time on the island. It was the first real vacation she'd had in years. After saying their farewells and boarding the yacht they arrived on, Xian did her best to let the ride back be filled with thoughts of the times she'd spent with Michael enjoying each other and not the battles which were just a few more miles away. Sensing she was getting nervous, Michael held her close as they watched the island get smaller and smaller until it was no longer visible. The sun was letting off some heat already, so they decided to go below and relax as best they could.

When they were below, she reached for him kissing him roughly. She wanted a distraction and none was better than him. Taking her cue, he pulled her towards the bedroom and did his best to make her forget everything waiting for them in Miami. For almost the entire trip they stayed in bed. They loved each other as if this would be their last time together. Not wanting to believe it, yet not wanting to take the chance of showing him how she felt, Xian let herself get lost in his embrace. Reacting to her, Michael didn't stop touching her until she held him close so he could no longer move. Smiling he kissed her forehead and relished the intimacy of just her holding tightly against him.

Being on the island not only allowed Xian to relax and recharge, it also heightened her awareness of the spiritual changes that continued to take place in Miami. The hairs on her body stood up as soon as her feet hit the dock.

"Is this how you feel when evil is around?" she asked Michael as they made their way towards her parked car.

"Yes but more intensely. It will serve you well; embrace it but don't let it create fear in your heart. Remember, fear is what feeds it."

Deciding to jump right in, Michael drove them to a location just outside the city limits in a small industrial park area. On the island, one of the angels told him about a new stronghold where newly possessed were being trained to fight. Figuring the variety of skill levels at this location would give Xian a good mix to fine tune her skills, Michael gave her a brief heads-up on what to expect, leaving out the part that they weren't fully trained to fight yet and their seasoned trainers would be there.

He parked a few buildings away from the one where the possessed were supposed to be. The day was turning into a real humid one, so he made sure Xian drank as much water as she could from some bottles he took off the yacht.

"You need to remember to always stay hydrated. Never get into a fight if you're not, but if you must make it quick. Whenever you use your skills, you're drawing a lot from your body, which is made up of about 60 percent water. Okay?"

"Okay, stay hydrated or make it quick. I'll remember."

They made their way towards the building, keeping to the shadows cast by the bright sunshine. Slowly they could hear fighting sounds along with cheering from a group of people.

"I want you to send flames to consume as many as you can. Let flames be the only weapon you use on them. Remember, give it all you have, this is for real."

Nodding her head as they approached the area where the sounds of fighting echoed from, Xian let her senses guide her. Her skin prickled as they got closer and by the time she took another six steps, movement came fast from her right side. Not having much time to brace for the oncoming attackers, she decided to just head straight for them. Her tactic worked as the small group created a whole just big enough for her to end up on the other side of them. Spinning around to push flames on them, she simultaneously scanned around her for others waiting for a chance to pounce. Xian could see Michael nearby dealing with stragglers having no trouble at all, taking literally one strike to end each one after the other. She grunted as he made it all look so easy. Being an angel she figured had its advantages in a fight.

Pleased with how she was handling her group, she decided to expand the range of her attacks. The commotion they'd caused had now drawn the attention of more possessed. Short of feeling like she was in an apocalyptic movie, Xian screamed at herself that this was happening live, no retakes, not cut. With the first crew down in agony from the consuming flames, she focused on a bunch now rushing her way. Her mind filled with the image of a fireball larger than the area they took up. The strength it took to keep it solid started to make her shake a little. Feeling she'd lose intensity in heat, she shrank it while making up the distance between them and just before it reached the leading female, she expanded the flames size; engulfing them all. Their screams caught the attention of someone perched on a balcony of the building over to her left. They stood up once the last of the screams had died down to a low whimper.

Michael noticed them too but stayed where he was. Understanding he was not going to help, Xian kept her eye on the figure as it jumped to the ground then slowly walked in her direction. It was a man dressed in blue jeans and a gray tank top. His hair was buzz cut and honey blonde. The eyes though, the closer he got she saw how they were nothing but black orbs. Teeth clenched, he continued to approach, once a few feet away he stopped. The moments of sizing each other up made Michael shift his weight on his feet. He knew this one was not a new recruit. The stench that emanated from him meant he had occupied for a long time. Then just as he expected without warning he was consumed with a bright red and blue flame. *Geez I didn't even see her blink. Scary little thing she's turning into, just glad she's on our side,* he thought as the shocked face man slowly dropped to his knees in front of her. He tried not to scream, but the flame was giving off so much heat even Michael could feel a bit of it where he stood.

No sooner did the blood curly sounds escape his lips, did another group coming charging from inside the building he'd jump down from. Instead of signaling for help, Xian braced for the oncoming bodies. Her mouth was almost dry and licking her lips she slowly closed her eyes and willed another flaming image in her mind. Not sure if she could take on this new bunch, she clenched her fists and gave it all she had. Only a few in the front got caught by the burning heat, the others behind them used their bodies as a shield wall until they were almost on her. Xian had nothing left in the tank; she was spent. She barely managed to pull her sword handle from her side trap and ignite its flaming blade. Swilling by pure instinct, she managed to take down the first five of them. The remaining four however, landed most of their blows, forcing her to begin retreating.

As much as he wanted to rescue her, Michael stood his ground. She had to learn how to get out of such situations alone. *One she shouldn't have gotten into in the first place*, he thought getting angry that she disobeyed the last thing he told her; never get dehydrated when fighting. He flinched as she took the last punch before another of the four started to raise their foot, aiming at her head, intending to stomp it hard. Michael leaned forward getting ready to move in, when a sudden blast of fire shot out of Xian's body from every direction. It was enough to burn the legs of them all; who'd by now had formed a circle around her fetal positioned frame. They all backed up as each became consumed by flames moving up their bodies. Michael looked back at Xian, she wasn't moving; she was too still.

While the screams of agony continued, he quickly scooped her up and headed for the car. Once he placed her on the back seat, he drove them as fast as he could back home. She was out cold. Her skin was dry, even with the humidity, she wasn't sweating. Shaking his head and biting his bottom lip, he rushed her into the bathroom standing with her under a lukewarm shower. No time for a glass of water from the kitchen so he opened her mouth so she could drink as the water splashed like a heavy rain. Slowly she stirred against him.

"I've got you. You're safe. Just let the water help you hydrate. Try not to speak until you down some liquids."

Without making a fuss, she stood there with him glad to be safe and trying hard to stay awake, but her body and mind defeated her will. It was evening when she woke; her head was hurting a bit and all attempts to raise it from the pillow failed.

"Just rest, I'm here. I know you don't feel well now, but just trust me. The next time you'll know better how to handle yourself. Sleep now," Michael said as he dabbed a cool cloth along her forehead. He watched her for a while to make sure she was sound asleep. Once satisfied, he went into the living room area and prayed. He was still working on keeping still and letting her fight for herself, but these emotions all mixed inside him were starting to cause real unrest.

"Father God, please help me to control my heart. Help me to be strong for her. I fear these human emotions will weaken my abilities where ever she's concerned. I cannot fail you; can't fail her."

As he knelt in front of the window a sweet peace came over him. His mind became clearer and heart light. He now understood that these very emotions are what he would need to not only connect with her, but protect her. Before he had no need for fear, for love on the level he loved her. His assignments were clean cut and nothing needed to be thought out, strategized; there was nothing to lose. Xian had taken his world and pulled it inside out. The physical bond they were developing he wore like a second skin. To not fail her meant he had to make sure she was equipped to handle whatever Satan threw at her. *As soon as she gets her strength back, I will do what I should have from the start. She needs a part of me to destroy anything or anyone that tries to take her out*, he thought as he rose to go back and check on her in the bedroom. She was still sleeping and when he touched her arm, her body temperature felt normal; her skin was subtle again. Relieved he went to the kitchen and ordered delivery. He knew she'd be famished whenever she finally woke. Maybe he should learn how to cook, they both loved good food and it could be another bonding experience for them. Tossing the idea around in his mind for a few minutes he shook it and laughed at himself.

"Yeah and then I'd be doing laundry next," he said to his reflection on the black shiny refrigerator door.

Carreau was sitting behind a large iron desk in his office. He liked to play boss, having an office space set the tone for his troops to stay in line. Spread out on the table was a map of the city. Areas were color coded as being either completely under his control, in the process of being taken over or those yet to get a taste of his power. Throughout the area, he had safe places the mass amount of demons waited for bodies to possess. Then there were the training facilities where they learned how to take control of their new meat suits. Similar to the one that he got a report on, which had been invaded by none other than Xian, the Sword of Vengeance and that pesky bulldog Michael. Those two were really getting under his skin. He called an urgent meeting with his troop leaders to come up with a plan to be rid of them both once and for all. There was a knock on the door, to which he beckoned the person to enter. The troop leaders single filed into the office. Signaling for them to sit, Carreau leaned back in his chair, looked each one in the eyes then started.

"I'm sure word has spread and you all know of the little untimely interruption to production we had at one of the training facilities. Needless to say, I don't want a repeat of this in my city. So, with that, I think it's time we throw these two bumps on my speedway a going away party."

The others nodded and mumbled their agreements to each other and Carreau. Not wanting to be the first to ask just what the plan was, each sat still in their chairs, attention now solely back on Carreau. He let the quiet grow to an almost deafening level in the room before he stood up and walked to a duplicate map of the one on his desk, hanging on the wall near the office door.

"We, my good people, have the opportunity to be number one in Satan's graces if we can get rid of these two. Everybody understands my meaning here?" he said slightly turning back towards them.

With a resounding yes, they all shifted a little to better face the map hanging on the wall. Taking a long bamboo rod from the umbrella basket near him, Carreau began to point out the areas of the city best to have the little send-off. Each had really good strategic points for attacking as well as the fact that there would be little to no unwanted onlookers stumbling upon the festivities.

"From my watchers Sir, the second location would be one most likely visited by them, since they frequent the shops nearby," said one of the troop leaders.

"Is that right? Well then, so be it. Get everyone ready, and I want only the strongest we have. Numbers are good but I need abilities to ensure the job is done right the first time. There will not be a second shot, got it?" he replied slapping the bamboo rod against the map while glaring at them all. In unison they agreed then left when he waved them towards the door.

This is the moment I've been waiting for. One hard strike and then I move to the top of Satan's list. I'll be second in command of this planet and all the weak minded trolls living on it, he thought as he took a seat behind his desk again. He'd been patient for a very long time, taking all the grunt work over the millennia. *Whatever I have to do now can't be worse than all I've already done. Besides I need to issue out some get back for all the headaches want to be big and mighty Michael and his short sidekick have given me lately. Yeah no way they are living through this beat down. This time next week I plan to be relocating to the top floor, penthouse style suites me better than basement living. Those other fools think I don't know how they look down at me. Azazel, Beelzebub, Dagon, Meresin and Verrine, Hmm all will be doing my bidding. Satan has other things to deal with so yeah, I definitely see them having to come begging me for a piece of the scraps I see fit to throw them.* Feeling full of himself, he looked over the map on his desk, mentally planning where he would build his new stronghold as second in command to Satan. *If I push hard, I can have it completed in about sixty days,* he thought as he let himself daydream turning to stare out the window.

As Carreau continued to live out his mental fantasy, Satan watched him from high above. Shaking his head he chuckled to himself. He wondered sometimes if those around him would ever really learn. *This world belongs to me and me alone. There were never any plans to share it with anyone, not even the one who created it. It was to be my prison, but instead I made it my kingdom. God has Heaven, I have Earth. The arrangement suits me just fine, at least until it no longer does. Carreau just like the others has lofty ambitions but neither one of them have the guts to actually do anything original as I did in Heaven that memorable day. So as long as they feel there is a chance, no matter how slight, they'd get to be more than what they already are, I will have a use for them. The day they're no longer useful, well for their sakes let's just hope they never feel there are no chances for them; wouldn't want to have to go recruiting for someone to fill in any sudden vacancies in leadership around here,* he thought, rubbing his chin as he let his gaze wander across the beautiful blue marble he held captive.

The sudden urge for female flesh sparked a wicked thought in him. It had been only a few hours since he last toyed with a few but he was bored now. All this thinking of discontent within his ranks made him want to take control of something. Something soft and pure, sweet and untouched by anyone else; a virgin was what he desired most right now. Sighing he walked across the sky. They were becoming harder to find these days; the truly pure ones. Never mind, something soft and sweet smelling regardless will do. A pity Xian wasn't so easily fooled by his charms. She was certainly easy on the eyes and underneath that tough shell, he really wondered what it took to get her going, as he fell towards the Earth's surface. Since having her was sure not to happen, he figured maybe he'd have a go at someone nearby. Landing on the busy streets of South Beach, he changed his appearance to that of a young man in swim shorts and flip flops. This time of day there were many almost naked women on the beach. Almost like going shopping for produce, the variety was just spread out for the picking.

Spotting a group of three giggling near a public shower, he approached plastering his irresistible smile on his face. *Eenie, meenie, miney, mo,* he thought as he looked from one to the other. Deciding on the middle one, he made his move. To his delight all three gave him strong vibes and their scents mixed for a lovely bouquet filling his nose. *All three it is then*, he smiled as they made their way back to the hotel a few blocks away the girls were staying at. *You got to love the groupies that share*, he said in his mind as he took in visually all they were so terrible at trying to cover up.

CHAPTER 17

After a long nap and several rounds of eating, Xian was back to feeling like herself again. Michael decided some fresh air would do her good and they needed to stock up on some of her favorite snacks, so a trip to the store was next on the agenda.

"So what about we try to make some of your favorite dishes instead of ordering out so much?" he said following her along the grocery store aisle.

"Wait, you want to cook now?" she asked stopping suddenly in front of the shopping cart he was pushing, almost getting run over.

"Yeah what's the big deal? I thought we could you know, bond more while we cooked. I mean it's like you're hungry every couple of hours like clockwork anyways."

"Right blame you're increasing love for food on me and my high metabolism," she replied over her shoulder reaching for a box of granola from a shelf that was just too high for her.

Without hesitation, Michael reached over her and got two boxes. Looking at her expression he said,

'Right, like one box will last more than two days around you."

Shaking her head and rolling her eyes she turned and continued down the aisle. The store was rather crowded that afternoon. Not wanting to be standing at check out any longer than necessary, Xian opted to not spend her usual extra time price comparing the fruit and picked up whatever looked fresh and juicy. Soon they were in a checkout line and as if on cue, hunger pains poke her gut. Michael just smiled at her when she glanced to see if he understood why she was rubbing her stomach.

"I'm not saying a word. Not a single one," he finally said picking up a magazine from a rack pretending to read it.

Walking in the parking lot, Xian had the feeling they were being watched and not just by a few people. It felt like everyone was getting in a few side glances at them.

"Yeah, we have company," Michael said confirming her suspicions, "just get in the car and pretend you don't notice."

They managed to get onto the side street without incident, to Xian's relief as she just wanted to get some food in her belly. Reaching into a bag on the back seat her hand felt an apple. She pulled it out and started to eat. It was nice and juicy. She had eaten half of it when the scenery outside the car let her know they were headed to the last stop of the shopping trip; the meat market. Her favorite butcher shop was just a few blocks away from the grocery store, but off the main road. By far they had the freshest cuts around the city and the fish was one of the main reasons she went there. Apparently they were supplied by local fishermen and hardly anything they sold was frozen. The traffic ahead caused them to slow down to a crawl. It looked like there was a detour just before their exit, which set off a little hissy fit in Xian.

 Deciding to just take a few deep breaths and enjoy being outside for a change instead of recovering in bed, she let her eyes take in the people passing on the nearby sidewalk. Everyone seemed to be going about their business; typical day in the city. Soon they were turning down a side street, following several other vehicles. They were about to approach the next turn to go left when several men dressed in construction hard hats and reflective vests, directed them to turn right instead.

 "Something is definitely up. We seem to be the only car detouring this way. Be ready for anything," Michael said softly as if the car had ears.

 Sitting up straight, Xian scanned the buildings as they drove past. She leaned back reaching into the bag of water bottles Michael left in the car when they got off the yacht. She downed a bottle in one go. No one seemed to be hanging around suspiciously but the hairs on her body screamed otherwise. Closing her eyes she scanned again. This time the number of possessed hiding inside buildings flanking the street made her gasp.

"Don't let the number knock you off your game. Focus on your techniques and you won't have to do much hand to hand fighting."

"You knew they were there. Why didn't you just tell me?" she asked trying to keep her voice calm but failing with each word.

"If I do everything for you, then I become a crutch you can't afford to have. You have all the skills necessary to defeat them Xian. Never doubt yourself otherwise you may as well not show up to the fight."

It was then that a large truck pulled across them, blocking the way forward. A glance in the rearview mirror confirmed Xian's fear, another truck had just parked behind them; there was no way left to drive out of this trap. Hearing Michael's words looping in her ears, she finished her apple and waited. In typical South Florida fashion, the not so long ago sunny skies were being overcast by several dark gray clouds. Since Michael wasn't saying anything, she closed her eyes again to see if there was any change in the crowd's formation. Something was happening because almost half were gone from either side. Michaels blue glow started to fill the car. He reached for her hand and squeezed it. Trying to choose his words carefully he opted to just lay it out for her, no need to sugar coat it now. He'd spotted Carreau on a building top just before the truck had blocked the road in front of them. This was not a training hideout or storage location, this was planned. He knew they were being watched and often wondered when somewhere they frequented would end up in and all-out battle. Regardless, he figured it would be easier if the fight was brought to them, so he let their routine go unchanged.

"Alright, any minute now, they will attack. We need to get out of this car. We'll stand in the front of it since the area is smaller making it more difficult for a large group to attack at once," he paused and turned more towards her holding her hand tighter, "I believe in you Xian. You have all you need inside to defeat them; just believe in the gifts inside you and trust that The Father will always make a way. As a last training giftr to you, I shared some of my energy with you a little while ago when you were dehydrated and sleeping. It will give you the extra boost you need when facing really large threats."

She nodded and started to lean in, but he moved back slightly. She smiled instead, realizing she almost gave away their secret. As far as the enemy knows, Michael has no real weaknesses. Their connection beyond that of teacher and student would be something used against him; worst used against her. As they stood back to back on the street, the sweet smell of rain passed overhead. Glad for the water to help keep her hydrated, Xian built a huge flame in her mind. She planned to let the first wave get it the instant they showed themselves; which happened to be now.

  The quiet was disrupted by a roar bursting from the shadows of the building in front of her. As planned, they were all consumed in flames. Almost at the same time they screamed, she could hear a similar roar at her back. Michael made quick dust of his group. Understanding not to take her eyes off her side of the street, she got ready for undoubtedly the next wave of attackers. Instead of a large group, fighters came at her one after another, with each doing their best to land kill shots. Reality check number one punched her brain hard so that Michael's words registered. Unless The Father prepared a way out of this fight, they were going to have to use every ounce of fight in them to stay alive. *No way am I dying today. I just got married to the most dreamy man, angel, whatever; acquired some Ma-*

trix-like skills and I'm still hungry, she thought to herself as she fought back.

Not wanting to waste energy, she used three or fewer moves per attacker. Some were faster than others, but if her sword didn't finish them, she resorted to fire. After about five minutes of nonstop hand to hand action, she shouted for Michael to brace himself. With that she sent out flames in all directions; bodies lighting up like drought withered trees. Only a few managed to let out screams as most were so quickly consumed they practically melted. Carreau had seen enough. The first two waves of attacks were destroyed within minutes and these were his best fighters. He couldn't afford for the remaining ones to get destroyed, so he signaled for them to fall back.

"I'll handle them myself," he said as he jumped down onto the street from the top of the building where he was viewing the action.

"I wondered when you'd join in the fun," Michael said in his direction as he walked closer to Xian. When they were next to each other, Carreau laughed,

"How cute is this? So are you going to have me fight against her? Really Michael? I thought you were the loaner type. Either way, neither one of you will be leaving here."

Leaning in closer to Xian's ear, Michael said,

"Don't listen to anything he says about you or me. He will try his best to make you doubt everything you know is true. He's a good fighter, but more about power than speed. Consuming him with flames will only slow him down; you'll need to use your sword to destroy him. One strike to his heart is all it'll take. Tap into all the power you hold inside."

"Are you two done strategizing? I have other things to take care of today; wait, where are you going Michael?" Carreau asked confused as Michael walked back towards the car.

"Oh I'm not going to fight you Carreau. Just as you guessed, she is," he said nodding in Xian's direction.

With disgusts now on his face, Carreau looked Xian up and down. She wasn't much of a fighter to look at but then again she just took out a lot of his best foot soldiers. Seeing she was not one to be underestimated, Carreau readied himself for whatever she was cooking up in her pretty little head. *I need to get him to attack me, and then I can plan my counter and take him out. I'm really not trying to have a long drawn out brawl with this one*, she thought. Her eyes though seemed to give away her thoughts as Carreau taunted her by saying,

"Oh come now sweetheart, you really don't think I'm going to go on the offensive with you, do you?"

Seeing he wasn't going to make the first move, Xian decided to start it off with a seemingly obvious charge. As expected, Carreau stepped aside but not before she was able to calculate just how slow his reaction timing was. She tested her theory with a few more charges then got ready to set him up on his over-confident approach. She played him like a chess piece, observing Michael was paying off. As he swung at her with a left jab, Xian rolled along the outside of his arm and when her back was to him, she quickly did a backward thrust of her blade in his heart. He had blinked so he missed the complete beauty of the move, but surely felt the heat of the blade burning him from inside out.

Michael's grin was huge as he watched her take Carreau down. He thought it would have lasted a little longer but he was happy and relieved it was over. *One down and much more to go*, he thought. To say Xian's confidence was up would have been an understatement. When the possessed still hiding in the buildings around them saw Carreau fall, then quickly disbursed. Xian looked at Michael as if to ask whether they were going to chase after them.

"No, others will take care of them. Your work is done for now in this city. As soon as Satan finds out what happened here, another will take Carreau's place, but before that happens, we need to raid all the locations he's been hiding his demons. Getting rid of those will hit Satan's plan hard. That's how we make a real difference. The rain began to fall and Xian smiled as she let some of if wet her down. It cooled her heated skin and she felt all the early anxieties roll off her with each cleansing drop.

CHAPTER 18

Xian's adrenaline was on overload. She could hardly keep still in her car seat on the drive back home. After they got there, Michael decided he would give cooking a simple pasta dish for them a try, since they didn't make it to the meat market. Figuring it couldn't be that difficult to follow the video streaming on Xian's tablet, he proceeded to chop up the few vegetable ingredients the recipe called for. Needing to do something with herself still, Xian worked on turning some sliced bread into buttery garlic bites. They didn't really speak; Michael decided to let her work through the mix of emotions she was feeling. When she was ready to talk, he'd listen.

The butter made her fingers slippery and she lost her grip of the baking sheet. In one twist of her hand, all the bread pieces tumbled onto the floor followed by the metal sheet, which sent a crashing sound throughout the small kitchen space. The tears flowed soon after. When he turned to see if she was alright, Michael quickly dropped the knife, dried his hands and pulled her close to him. By this time she was shaking uncontrollably and no matter how she tried to formulate words, they just came out as stammering gasps of air.

"Let it out my love. It's okay. You're safe now," he softly said trying to reassure her that the danger was passed. He knew firsthand how emotions can flip your world around quickly but never had he experienced anything she was going through because of a fight. *You idiot, fighting is all you know. She just had her life dissected and told she was the center of some super heavy supernatural battle that's been going on for ages,* his mind screamed, *don't just stand there holding her like a pet, make her stop crying. Distract her genius.*

    The only thing he wanted to do was make her feel better. With one hand he reached over and stopped the video playing on the tablet, then turned off the stove. Picking her up bridal style he carried her to the bedroom. Her hair was a big puff of loose curls making her look so much younger than she was. Swollen, wet eyes looked back at him; he was done. She had control over him that made him lose the little grip he had on his senses. Her lips pulled him in like a super magnet. His kiss was gentle then it got stronger as he stripped off her clothes. Before he could undress she pushed his hands away and did it herself. That was the first time she controlled the bedroom, taking all the frustration, fear and excitement she felt out on him. If their bond could get any closer, he didn't see how. For her he would do anything, he wondered if she felt the same.

When they finally decided what to eat for dinner, it was agreed pizza would do. Michael's culinary attempt was scrapped for another time. They exchanged small talk not really touching anything too sensitive, almost as if it were on a first date and neither knew where the line was drawn. *You have to talk to him sooner or later. Why are you acting like he did something wrong? You knew that he was meant to train you, not do the fighting for you. Get a grip, can't you see he's confused. Poor thing doesn't know what to say or do, afraid you'll become another puddle of tears. Shut down the pity party and love on this fine heart beat in front of you before you regret shutting him out*, her inner voice spat at her.

Xian gave Michael a small sincere smile, her eyes slowly losing their sadness the longer she looked at him,

"I'm sorry. I just had an emotion overdose. Realizing that fight could have been the end of us really shook me to the core. I don't know how I'd live without you in this new reality of mine. Know that I do love you and I'd do anything for you as I know you'd do anything for me," she said as walked over towards him spread out on the sofa. He sat up as she got near, not sure what to say, not wanting to ruin the moment; so he just watched her. Slowly his true form came forward and his eyes turned blue, the light shade she had grown to love. His energy surrounded them like a shield. With her eyes closed she was able to see him better, only this time she felt him reach into her, touching her spirit with his, but only for a brief moment. Then he let her go,

drifting back into his human body.

"What was that?" she asked while trying to catch her breath. The experience gave her sensations she couldn't begin to describe.

"I wanted you to really feel me if only once. Do you still love me Xian, or is it this body that you are drawn to?" Michael asked his voice low and uncertain.

Touching his face as she bent before him, she kissed him softly then pulled away just far enough for them to look each other in the eyes before she replied,

"This body I touch is just a shell that you control. It's you who makes these hands hold me, these lips kiss me, this heart love me; just as my spirit controls my body. When you took me to train in the gated community soon after we met and I saw sparing, revealing your true self to me, from that moment you had me. You are the most wonderful person I've ever known, angel or not. You gave up your life in Heaven for me, seriously what more can a girl ask for?" she said trying to lighten the heavy mood.

Finally Michael let out the breath he'd been holding. His heart beats were still pretty hard in his chest. He had to shake off all the energy still wanting to break free. He needed to fly. Grabbing her hand he took her out the apartment and before she could accept or decline, they were shooting up into the night's sky. Holding her tight he soared as high as he dared without freaking her out more than she already was. He knew heights were not her thing, but she didn't complain, just held onto him and peeked every so often between her tightly closed eyes at him. When he told her to look around she just smiled and squeezed them tighter.

"Okay, I appreciate you coming with me and I don't want you to have another panic attack," he said jokingly, "let's go back home."

The rest of that week, Michael explained to Xian the key players in Satan's plan to control the city. Bishop Thomas Strickman, who was the means that Carreau used to get people for his demons to possess, mainly he funneled the lost and desperate member of his mega-church in exchange for being the largest church in the city and to keep his homosexual secrets just that, a secret. Jeremy and Leanne Mitchell, the once connected fraternity and sorority pledged couple from Chicago. They landed in Miami with the hopes to reclaim their lost status in society along with the hundreds of thousands of dollars swindled, then lost by shady business deals and questionable life choices. Currently they were making plans to connect with Bishop Strickman to use his large congregation network to promote false plans of instant wealth using cleverly camouflaged pyramid schemes. Their other agenda was to scout out new members to join their secret organizations, setting up a continuous income stream from membership dues. What the members wouldn't know until it was too late, was that the Mitchells were not connecting them to their orders back in Chicago, but were setting up their own here in Miami from which they planned to undermine the ones in Chicago that ran them out of town; causing them to lose everything. Of course Satan has his hand on their lives since the day they took their first pledge back in college. So yes, they to are recruiting souls for him.

Leaving the dearest to Satan's heart for the last, he mentioned Richard and Jenny.

"You understand that everything The Father has done, Satan has introduced his own twisted and perverted version, right? Well Richard and Jenny represent his Adam and Eve in this city. His plan is to use them to lead the lost to a false salvation, and then open them up for possession. From what I understand, both of them have been under Satan's thumb from early childhood. They have mentally been conditioned to serve him; I'm really not sure how much of their own free will remains."

"So am I supposed to fight these people like the other possessed?"

"No not fight as with the others. You are to show them the path to true deliverance. Honestly, fighting the possessed compared to dealing with these people is a walk in the park. Each one has some serious issues and a lot of self-hate. To battle them, you'll need to learn how to sever them from the hold Satan himself has on them. You'll have to learn how to deliver them while keeping their memories intake, of what it is they've been delivered from. So far you have been destroying the single demons of possessed people who in the end don't remember anything once free. These people are being mentally controlled by Satan, meaning they have many demons possessing them. Also, these he won't give up control over so easily.

"I don't see how I'm supposed to help them find real deliverance. I mean what technique am I to use on them?"

"The Father himself my love, will provide the means necessary. You just need to stay prayed up and focused on the task at hand."

"So what, no more fighting; I just wait around for The Father to equip me?"

"Hmm not exactly, I mean there will be fighting but as for the waiting around The Father has already started to equip you," he said with a raised eyebrow and half-smile. Seeing she was still confused he added,

"While you're sleeping my dear, The Father is talking to your spirit. Don't worry, when the time comes to begin the next stage of your mission, He will let you know. In the meantime, when you wake up immediately recall your dreams. In them lie the keys to unlock whatever He has placed in you through the night."

Over the next few weeks, Xian and Michael raided every location known to be a place where the possessed trained and where demons waited for host bodies. They struck whenever a location was most active, regardless what time of day it was. Xian's skills had greatly improved. Michael often joked that he was just her personal chauffer and shopping assistant. Every time he pretended to feel unneeded and left out the fighting action, she gave him a hug and kiss; reassuring him just how needed he was.

Satan had decided to handle Miami himself and this left his generals wondering just what was so important about that city. Not wanting to be the one to question his decisions, none dared to say anything. He had practically relocated to Miami Beach surrounded by an endless supply of women, no ethnicity went unrepresented. Since Carreau had already done a good job organizing the local troops, it was easy for Satan to step in and keep the possession schedule on track. Jenny was proving to be a useful tool as he expected. She had Richard wrapped around her fingers. He was so hooked on her body, getting him to continue branding the new recruits was no longer an issue.

Jenny was simple enough to keep motivated. A luxurious lifestyle was all she really wanted and having Richard practically worshiping her was the only other thing necessary to keep her in line. Their penthouse was a constant buzz of information. The local businessmen and politicians, practically lined up to rub shoulders with the suddenly most powerful couple in the area. No one really knew who they were or how they'd become so influential, just that almost overnight they were the ones you had to know in order to get ahead.

A rainbow appeared in the sky and Satan gazed at if from his balcony. The symbol mocked him until his temper nearly overtook him. Soon this place and all on the Earth would be burned in the fire God promised to send. His time was winding up and still he had many souls to capture. His end game was soon going to be played out and his numbers still weren't as high as he wanted. Letting out a sigh, he went back inside the penthouse waving his hand at the beauties littered throughout the living room space. He motioned for them to leave him alone. He needed to think and all they were doing was distracting him. If he pushed harder on Bishop Strickman, the numbers could increase some over the next quarter, but having more than Strickman as a pipeline, he'd see the numbers really rise. He mentally summoned one of the assistants staying with him.

"Yes Sir, you called?"

"Find out who the hungry up and coming preachers are in the city. Also, while you're at it connect me to the Mayor; I want to introduce myself."

"Yes Sir, right away Sir," the assistant replied as

he turned and left Satan to his thoughts.

Yeah, more pipelines are what I need. Never know when the old man will call checkmate and I can't afford to be shorthanded on my soul count; the ultimate spiritual bargaining chip.

After another hour passed, the assistant came back to where Satan was relaxing in the large loveseat.

"Sir, you have a meeting with the Mayor this afternoon at 3:30 p.m. As for the list of hungry up and coming preachers in the area, I have a list here for your review," he said holding a single sheet of paper in his hands.

Holding out his hands to receive it Satan replied,

"Wonderful, have the car ready to take me around 2:00 p.m. I don't want to risk being late; shouldn't keep someone as important as the Mayor waiting, now should we?"

"No Sir, we shouldn't. The car will be waiting downstairs before 2:00 p.m. Is there anything else I can get you?"

"No that will be all for now," he mumbled as he studied the names listed on the paper. Three names jumped out at him at first glance. He'd had his minions watching them for years. Smiling he began to formulate a plan. Based on their addresses, they were conveniently scattered around town. This was going to be easier than he thought. The future was definitely looking up. *Loosing Carreau may not have been a bad thing after all,* he thought, *yes there are opportunities everywhere if you just look hard enough. Hmm I still have an extra hour to kill before I get ready to meet the driver, time to see just what my lovely companions have gotten themselves into.*

"Oh ladies, where have you all gotten to, Hmm?" he called out as he made his way down the long corridor flanked by bedrooms.

At 3:30 p.m. Satan was sitting in the office of the city's Mayor. Small pleasantries were exchanged and then he got straight to the point.

"Mayor I feel that we both can benefit from a proposition I have. Word on the street is that your supporters over on the West Side have decided to back your main opponent in this year's upcoming re-elections. Overall you've done wonders for this city; it would be a shame for many initiatives you've started to not see fruition."

"Yes well I'm doing all I can for the West Side but it's somewhat of a challenge when landowners in that area won't cooperate with revitalization projects and giving public access to a better transportation system in and out of that area. Just how is it that you can help me?"

Smiling now with laced fingers in front of his chest Satan replied,

"I happen to be the majority landowner in the area. Nothing gets done on the West Side without my consent. You see Mayor; I've been waiting for the right opportunity to present itself that would, let's say, solidify my holdings in this entire area."

"Oh and just what opportunity are you referring to?" the Mayor replied giving Satan is full attention, slightly leaning forward on his desk.

"To be frank, the opportunity to assist a certain political figure with his past; recreating a new life takes a lot of money and connections. Both, I happen to have in abundance. South America maybe far away, but the reach of those in power there can come as close as your home's front door, if you get my meaning?"

With a slightly bowed head and eyes showing defeat, the Mayor nodded. He had wondered how long it would be before someone found out the truth about him. His life these past 20 years had been filled with a lot of anxiety. Escaping forever the blood ties of his youth was almost next to impossible; but he had hoped somehow he would.

"What exactly is it you can do for me and what in return am I supposed to give you?"

"Oh I can make it all disappear, my friend. Can I call you friend? Titles only seems fitting now that we are getting into bed together as it were. By this time next week you could be remembered as only the man you turned yourself into. No one will remember the man who walked away from the underworld of South America just when he was sitting on the top of it. Besides, you're leaving made many extremely rich and powerful. Honestly they saw it as a blessing for them. Still a few harbor resentment for leaving them in life and death situations. Many were tortured and mutilated on suspicion alone of helping you flee."

The Mayor closed his eyes as he tried to shut out the images of his friends and associates who undoubtedly suffered because of his decision to leave South America.

More often than he could count, their faces cried out to him in his dreams. Now he was to trade favors with another powerful man in order to continue living in his glass house. The picture of his family stared back at him from the corner of his desk. For them he would endure any hell. It was only because of them was he able to forgive himself for all the horrors he'd done so long ago.

"Fine, just tell me what you need from me?"

"Oh it's nothing that difficult actually. I just need your soul," Satan said letting his eyes turn into black pools while he grinned, exposing gleaming white teeth.

CHAPTER 19

Xian's started to have more vivid dreams. Each one would repeat itself for three nights then another one would begin. As Michael had said, she immediately recalled them upon waking. She was getting really good at deciphering the meanings and how to help the others gain real deliverance from Satan. Michael did his best to keep her physically in shape. Besides raiding hideouts, they started to have more intense workouts with the others in the gated community he first trained her at. Lately it seemed like they'd all but moved in. Though it was a great cover, Xian and Michael preferred to stay in the city. Overall, it suited them more.

To switch things up, he decided they would go and take some cooking classes together. Xian he knew could manage some tasty meals, but he wanted them to still try and have some type of a normalcy to their marriage regardless of what was going on around them. She was actually excited about taking the classes. He hoped though she also wanted to escape and just be with him doing everyday things other couples did. Another great thing about taking the classes was that they'd get to bring home the meals prepared. The idea of having something new and different to eat was another key selling point of the plan.

After the third class, Michael walked around the kitchen like he was some world class chef. Xian decided to feed his ego further and purchased a chef's hat and a monogrammed apron for him. He was over the moon in appreciation of the gifts. *I could just stay this way forever with him; well minus the fighting and city in peril stuff. Ahh who am I kidding, that's part of what bonds us even more,* she said to herself, smiling at the last part while she drew finger swirls on the countertop. Regardless if he was busy doing something, Michael never missed the little things she did. He couldn't read her mind, but he could tell from her face and relaxed posture she was in a good place emotionally. This made him relax a bit. They worked hard to make their home a place of retreat. Even the mention of getting a dog came up a few times. Yet they were both just too selfish with each other to share their love and time.

"We've become such an old loving couple," Xian said as she continued to draw on the countertop with her finger.

Not looking up from the cutting board as he continued to dice vegetables Michael replied,

"Yes indeed; loving every single minute of it, aren't you?"

"Every single minute," she said now looking up at him with a big tooth-filled smile.

Thinking it was a good time to coax her to open up a little about what she'd been dreaming lately Michael took a stab at it by casually asking while he grabbed another pot from the drawer at his feet.

"So any direction we're supposed to take from your dreams yet?"

"Hmm well mostly it's been about me and building my faith. I need to have the kind, you know like you do. You never question if you do something will it be successful or not. I guess what it is I'm trying to say is my dreams showed me to build up blind faith. I can't go after these people second guessing anything."

"I understand. For me there was nothing other than The Fathers word to hold onto. Humans are bombarded with so much information and lots of choices over the course of their lives that holding onto something they can't see requires some major reprogramming."

"Yeah but at least I have you. You are a constant reminder to me that my faith is founded in someone real. Okay enough about that, how much longer before we eat, I'm starving?"

Laughing at her exaggerated hungry expression, Michael handed her a few slices of apple and a handful of walnuts he was using for the side salad.

"Here, munch on these greedy. Are you sure you don't have worms?" he said trying hard to keep a straight face.

"What, how can you think such a thing? I don't have worms, just a..."

"High metabolism," they both said in unison. Michael more in a mocking tone as this was Xian's excuse whenever she gave the reason for her constant snacking.

That night her dream was different. It felt so real she wasn't sure if she was really asleep. It was night time and she was walking up a hill at the edge of a city. She couldn't make out the city in particular nor did the place she walked seem familiar. When she got to the top of the hill her feet started to leave the ground. Slowly she rose upward, but she wasn't afraid of being so high in the air. That was the clue that made her realize this was definitely a dream. Then there was a voice, it was deep and strong. It comforted her more as the city suddenly became ablaze. Red, black and orange were the only colors the buildings now were. Though there should have been unbearable heat rising from them, she felt nothing but a soft cool breeze.

"This is what is to come for this world. Many refuse me and cling to the illusion that Satan continues to provide for them. You have a charge to reach and save as many of these lost souls as you can in your lifetime. Your faith in me and desire to serve is the reason I've chosen you, but you are not the only one."

"Not the only one?" She asked.

"You will never leave me as I will never leave you. Every test, you have passed despite many harsh obstacles you have yielded yourself to my will. No man is perfect but you have shown yourself worthy of the tasks ahead. Your faith is the key that will unlock all the doors to my kingdom Xian. Use it even when your eyes can't see the outcome. Even when your heart feels like it will shatter and never be whole again. Remember as my Word says, I will never leave you nor forsake you my child."

The words branded themselves along with the images she saw in her heart. So many needed to be reached and though the time when this burning fire would happen wasn't revealed, she knew that it was soon to come. Her eyes flew open, she was now awake. Michael instinctively pulled her closer, but said nothing. He knew she needed time to process her thoughts so he let her be. Xian replayed the dream several times over, then rolled over and nuzzled her face against Michael's chest. His heartbeat lulled her back to sleep eventually. She felt safe next to him which made it easier to relax. Often after a dream her senses were so heightened that she had a difficult time relaxing. He benefited her in so many ways. She made a mental note to thank him again in the morning just as she drifted off.

The morning felt like it came only after a few minutes of resting to Xian. Michael was already dressed and holding a tray of food near the bedroom door. One look told her, they were not going to be hanging around the house much this morning. With a sigh she threw back the covers and motioned for him to rest the tray on the dresser as she headed for the bathroom. Apparently while she slept in the early morning hours, Michael was having a conversation in the living room with a pair of angels who were posted to the West Side of the city. Satan himself was in town. Xian almost choked on her toast when he told her.

"What do you mean exactly, Satan is in town?"

"It means he has not replaced Carreau and is handling things personally. Not really his thing but he is known to be irrational at times. As soon as you're ready, we're going to meet up with some other angels assigned to this city to discuss patterns in his operations movements of late."

Forty-five minutes later they were heading north towards the meet-up location. When they entered what looked like an old-fashioned diner, Xian followed Michael to a pair of double doors. Once on the other side he held her tight as the stomach to the throat feeling of suddenly dropping at great speeds made her clawed at his shoulders.

"Ah don't ever do that again without warning, okay?" she gasped once her feet were stable again on solid ground. Looking around she saw they were in a brightly lit tunnel. She followed him as he turned a bend which opened up into a large room, already filled with a few hundred people. After closer examination, she noticed they were actual angels, disguised like Michael.

"Okay great, you're here. Let's get started shall we?" said a man at the farthest side of the room.

"As you all know, there has been an opening in Satan's leadership thanks to Xian here. Now we all understand that this city is a gateway to Latin America and the Caribbean for Satan and his minions. The human soul trade is alive and well here and as such, it would appear that Satan himself is taking over the operation. Yesterday he was seen leaving the Mayor's office and from our sources, the Mayor has been seeking allies to assist in affirming his re-election. From our brothers watching the West Side area, there has been a lot of demonic activity there. Many of the abandoned buildings in the old warehouse district have been getting regular deliveries and pickups, the majoring by trailer trucks. We all know what this means. Something huge is about to burst onto this city and we need to be prepared. Also, don't look for Satan to directly do anything, but understand he is surely the one pulling the strings."

"Based on our analysis of the past six months," said another man just to the left of the first speaker, "a constant large number of people are seen coming into the area late at night. Almost the same amount that goes to the Beaches for partying on the weekend, but the West Side has no clubs or nightlife to speak of. So my question is what is it all these people from different backgrounds and areas across two counties have in common? What is drawing them to this area in particular?"

"I think I can answer those questions for you," Michael said, still at the back of the room. Everyone who was facing forward, turned towards him.

"They are being branded. The lure that's used is the chance to connect with the in crowd; Miami's elite who themselves are in attendance during these gatherings."

"Branded?" someone deep in the crowd asked, "Really? There hasn't been any branding for almost a century."

"With the age we live in full of instant information, people are able to make choices more easily. Google and Wikipedia provide sources that unlock mysteries that no one a thousand years ago would ever question. Branding means he can bind them without the fear of them rejecting his minions when possession takes place. Free will works two ways, for or against. Besides, he's playing the numbers game. For everyone that comes to the light, he works hard to pull double into the dark with him."

"Do we know who Satan is using to brand these people?" said another voice from the far right of the room.

"Yes," said Michael, "and he is our assignment. What we could use from everyone else is information and help to stop the inflow of recruits as best you can. We need time and opportunity to get to this Brander, which means we need Satan's focus on incidents disrupting his operation. Understood?"

"Understood," they all said together.

With that Michael turned and walked back towards where they dropped down into the tunnel. Xian followed still not saying a word but processing what she just learned. Trying to piece together just how this information could help her get to Richard. Looking at him with a wary eye, she held him tight as the shot up the opening, landing back behind the double doors.

For the rest of the afternoon, he had her train. They worked on fine tuning some of her moves and then her speed. Michael held back less after each round. For a human she was really fast. This would be her advantage in every fight as it wouldn't be expected. Her stature and being a female made her opponents underestimate her; and she played off of that very well. Afterward they decided to grab a bite to eat on the way over to the West Side. Xian wanted to see just what everyone was talking about and Michael agreed a little reconnaissance of their own was in order.

They waited around the house until it was about after 10:00 p.m. Deciding to park at the train station nearest to the location they were checking out, they casually mingled with a group heading in the same direction. Slowly the group got bigger and the conversations started to get quite interesting.

"Yeah I just got an email for a chance to win a ticket to some exclusive party full of VIP's. Thinking I wouldn't really win, sent in my information and within the next few days the ticket was in my mailbox."

"Wow yeah the same thing happened to me and my cousin."

"I got mine from one of the waiters at a cafe near my job downtown. He said he gets a lot to give away as promos from his inside connection."

Looking at each other Michael and Xian slowly dropped back once the entrance of the building where the gathering was taking place came into view. Using the shadows as cover, they weaved their way across the backs of buildings until finding a side door to the one everyone filed into. Muffled voices over club music were coming from the room next to where they were. Little slits of light beamed through cracked plaster on the far wall. One quick short punch from Michael created a nice hole for them to peek through. On the other side they could see people drinking and dancing. Some were standing around laughing and talking while others were posted up like security.

Michael tapped her shoulder pointing at a line of people leading towards a set of drawn heavy red drapes. One by one they entered, exiting a few feet down from another guarded opening.

"That's where whatever these are really, about is going on," he said as he searched the wall for another spot to peak through. Finding one he motioned for her to follow him.

What they saw made Xian have to swallow down hard the bile that threatened to come out. Richard was putting brands on people two at a time. When they moved away, small red burn marks were on their skin. When they said branding, they meant exactly that. Standing next to him was a pale freckled face woman. She had a crazy look in her eyes. Chills went up Xian's spine just looking at her. After each person was branded they turned to her and bowed. She was eating it all up; definitely power hungry.

"We need to follow the newly branded to see where they go from here," Michael whispered. They observed the rest of the crowd from their first hole Michael had created. After an hour they spotted the Mayor talking to some of the others, and then Xian did a double take at the fine specimen that approached the Mayor from behind the red curtain. He was gorgeous. His suit was obviously custom made as it fit like a glove. His hair was platinum blonde and he wasn't as muscular as Michael, but he was just as tall and fit.

Michael pretended not to notice her reaction to Satan; instead he focused on the two and eavesdropped on the conversation. Apparently the Mayor was getting acquainted with his new political backer and then there was something about the deal made earlier that needed to be completed. Satan turned, followed by the Mayor, walking back behind the red curtain. Michael and Xian rushed back to the other peephole and watched as Richard branded the Mayor. While he bowed in front of Jenny, she seductively pulled his chin up so that she could stare into his eyes. Her eyes changed into black pools and as if under some spell, the Mayor reached up for her head, hungrily kissing her. What followed next was certainly Satan's extra blackmail insurance; branded women came and joined in with Jenny and the Mayor. Cameras flashed around them as the clothes started to come off. Michael picked up someone saying the first truck was loaded and ready to go.

"Let's go, they're on the move."

Quickly, they made their way outside just in time to see the back of the truck closing. Inside pressed close together were people Richard had branded. Figuring they wouldn't be able to go back for the car, Michael said he'd follow and phone Xian the directions so she could drive the car to the destination. As soon as the truck was over a block away, Michael took flight trailing the moving truck along several barely lit streets. It ended up only going about ten blocks before backing up to the loading dock of what looked like a cement manufacturing company. *Whatever they're doing, the noise of the factory gave good sound coverage*, he thought.

He called Xian and gave her the address. She was there after a few minutes. Sneaking into the front side of the building, they snooped around the office until Michael found what he was looking for. It was the biggest office off to the right. From the size and furnishing, it must belong to someone in charge. Xian turned on the computer but it was password protected. Michael touched the hard drive with his finger, and then presto, she was in. She searched folders and emails looking for any connection to what was happening. Nothing, it all looked like legitimate business stuff to her.

"I can't find anything out of the ordinary," she said standing up from the desk.

Michael slowly looked around the room as if looking into the walls. He stopped at the bookcase near the back wall. Fourth shelf down, the third book from the left, he pulled it out. Reaching into space it was covering, he flicked a switch and a hidden door cracked open behind the desk. *This is some straight spy movie foolishness*, Xian thought glancing at Michael. He walked to the door, slowly opening it and instantly a light came on in the small space. Inside they found a supply of drugs all packaged for distribution, from pills to weed to cocaine. Closing the door, Michael walked out the office, leading them towards the loading bay where the truck had parked earlier.

The last of the people were being ushered further into the plant. Fluorescent lighting dimly lit the way and as if in a trance the people quietly followed the person in front of them. The path ended at a big sliding metal door. Groups of no more than six were let in. What Michael saw on the other side made him finally reveal to Xian what he suspected,

"The manager is selling drugs based on his supply closet. In exchange to operate in this area, Satan gets to use this facility as a cover for possessing the newly branded people. I'll bet that from here they go to a training facility where the demons learn to fight in their host bodies and integrate into society, if the possession doesn't kill the host first."

"I see, so you're saying Richard then is the key and if we get rid of him we can stop this cycle?"

"We can slow it down. Satan will just find someone to take his place. It's really not about stopping Satan, but taking back the souls he's latched onto."

"But I thought that's why you've been training me, to fight Satan and his generals. To take back this city; what did I miss?"

Sighing he held her shoulders as if bracing her for an oncoming punch. He knew she didn't fully get the big picture since he gave her only what she could handle and only what was relevant at the time. He smiled as warmly as he could then said,

"You were to be trained to fight the demons possessing the people of this city. Take out any of the generals that got in your way. Destroy any minions you came across waiting for a host body. Satan is out of your league my sweet. He was never on the calling card for you."

"So who gets to take him out, you?"

"I doubt it. The Father has a plan and only he knows when it will be executed. I like my brothers follow orders and keep fighting so that things remain a certain balance. There are many people left who truly believe and need protecting from the leach claws of Satan and his followers. Your honor is great Xian. Of all the people in this city, you were chosen to be a defender of their faith, their right to choose a side in this fight. These people here are lost and because they chose material wealth and fame; things of this world, they are now about to embark on a horrific journey. This is what he's good at, spinning the truth, feeding into people's selfish desires."

Tears rolled down her face from gratitude that she was not one of those lost souls. She knew both sides of this war and her heart broke thinking of all who were being lured into the traps Satan constantly set for them until they took the bait. Pulling herself together, she looked back at the line of people slowly get smaller.

"So what do we do about them?"

"What we were commissioned to, deliver them," Michael said as he made an extended bow and hand wave in front of her as if to say after you. What happened next was an almost ballet of swords play. Xian mixed strikes and kicks to take out the few guards that were hanging around the loading dock. Even with all the commotion, those branded ones waited in line. Deciding to just be done with the room full of demons all at once, as soon as Michael slid back the metal door she released a flame that filled it in seconds. The smoke and screams were left trapped when he slid the door close again. Deciding to just free the ones already possessed, Xian went after them while Michael tended to the branded few remaining. He placed is hands on their brands and let his energy melt them away. Once the brands were gone, the people started to come out of their haze mind state, looking around confused.

"We have to get them help," Xian said, "what about just taking them back to the train station or at least to a more public place and get them some cabs, something?"

"Good ideas but not the best in this situation. Don't worry my sweet; I already called in the cavalry."

Soon after a group of the angels that they met earlier showed up. Each took a few with them in cars and assured Xian and Michael they'd get home safe without any memory of what happened tonight. Exhausted Xian leaned against him as they watched the last pile into a car. Knowing she'd had a long day, Michael swooped her up and carried her to where she stashed her car on the other side of the building. Glad that her feet didn't have to make the trek, Xian rested her head on his shoulder.

When they got home all she could manage was a quick shower and stuffing a few mouthfuls of leftovers in her before she was out cold. Michael just shook his head at how she laid sideways half off the bed. She looked like a little girl when she slept. Gently moving her to lay properly, he suddenly remembered the way her face lit up when she saw Satan. He shouldn't let it get to him since it was the reaction every woman had that ever had the chance to see him. He was made the most beautiful; all the angels knew this. Still the one who held his heart, her reaction stirred him and not in a good way. *Did she desire him? Is she dreaming of him now? Ahh genius, she didn't know who she was looking at. Try asking her when she wakes up, just duck from the head punch she's going to give you,* he thought before making himself comfortable next to her.

CHAPTER 20

Xian's dream started almost immediately once she lied on the bed. She barely felt when Michael shifted her. The dream started out her being in a crowded place, looked almost like a shopping mall food court. Food, even in her dreams she got hungry. Then the scene changed and she was hovering over the Earth looking down, standing next to the gorgeous blond man she saw talking with the Mayor. He was walking back and forth talking to several other men who were all dressed in armor as if going off to fight in a war. She couldn't hear well what they were saying but the way the men kept their heads bowed at Blonde, made her wonder who he was. Then she heard her name come from his lips. She strained hard to see if she could hear more and just like turning up the volume on a pair of speakers, she heard them.

"Nothing has changed. You all know what you're to do in your designated areas. I'll accept no delays in production, got it?"

"Got it"

"Now leave me. I have things to take care of personally."

Xian watched as the men bowed deeper before flying off the same way Michael did. A lump caught in her throat and she again felt bile creeping up from her stomach. The blonde man she was so taken by was Satan himself. How could she not have guessed and why didn't Michael tell her. *Oh no he must have felt so betrayed by the way I carried on when I saw him. I bet my face was just dripping with lust. Oh baby*! she thought wanting to kick herself for hurting him. She hadn't noticed from her sudden self-scolding that Satan had stopped pacing and was now looking at her. *Can he actually see me? This is a dream, right? Okay, weird!* She thought as she moved around to see if his eyes would follow her; they did. Taking a chance that they could actually communicate she tried speaking, but her voice was stopped by an unseen hand, she could only feel it covering her mouth. Understanding her confusion, Satan spoke instead,

"Hello Xian, nice to meet you, so to speak. Don't worry I can't touch you if that's what you're worried about. However, I know you can hear my words and yes I can see you, well a reflection of you at least."

Xian just stood there looking at him. Not sure what to do, she decided to just observe. There was a clue here somewhere that The Father wanted her to see. Something useful in freeing Richard and all the others was here and she had to find out what it was. He walked along the sky as if strolling in a field of flowers, his hands touching imaginary buds shooting up from the ground. This time he wore only flowing white pants, the fabric was light and flowed slightly behind him. His chest was bare and his hair hung long down his back; glistening. His eyes were not really a color, more iridescent, capturing little specs of color from his surroundings. He paused then spun around gazing at her again.

Xian had to admit, he worked his stuff better than any model or actor she knew. Everything about him oozed charm and finesse. His face had a slight smile growing wider the longer he looked at her. He let his gaze fall along the length of her body, and then slowly he let it rise up to her face again. *He's not flirting with you idiot, he's sizing you up*, she thought.

"Since I'm the only one with a voice here, I'll go ahead and do all the talking. I guess you've figured out who I am. Well as you can see I have not tail or horns for that matter, also no pitchfork. What I do have though are my wits and charm, both I can tell you're attracted to. Am I right? You can just nod."

Xian remained completely still. She wasn't sure whose hand was keeping her silent but for once she was glad for the muzzle. Michael's words kept repeating in her ears, she was no match for him and this is just what he does, mind games. Seeing she wasn't going to play along, Satan decided to try another tactic.

"I see you and my brother Michael are making a hell of a team. Yes, you two have caused me some setbacks but don't fret I have other means to make up for what I've lost. So, you are the Sword of Vengeance. Well I've learned a lifetime ago not to judge the outward appearance. It's all about what's on the inside, wouldn't you agree? I mean look at you, not much meat on the bones, not to tall either, but you have the "it" factor. I see why Father picked you. Even from your eyes I can tell right now if you could reach me, you'd certainly give it a shot. You've got drive; something I find that mankind has begun to lack over these last few hundred years. Everyone wants things now. None of them really want to earn anything. Yet I shouldn't complain, their impatience fuels my business," he said now standing closer to her, "you see darling, I know what you're planning to do, trust me it won't work. I own that city; I own this planet. This is my kingdom."

At this point Xian was sure if they were actually in the same space she would be able to feel his breath on her face, that's how close he'd gotten.

"This one-sided conversation is starting to bore me. What's the point of you seeing me if you can't at least say hello?" he said throwing up his hands as he turned and walked away.

"There, did you catch that," a voice whispered in her right ear, "did you see how quickly he becomes impatient?"

Nodding her head she continues to stare at the back of Satan's head. He was acting like a spoiled brat who couldn't have his way. Though he was trying to appear calm, his hands and the veins in his body were starting to rise. He spun around and faced her only this time he looked different. His body was no longer covered in the smooth creamy skin as before but by burned and peeling flesh. His gleaming blonde hair was now gone, exposing a skull with chunks of missing flesh. Eyes black as coal looked at her with a questioning expression. *What's wrong with her? Something's changed in her eyes, they're slightly wider than before*, he thought.

"This is what he really looks like, never forget it. He is the master of illusion and the sooner you get this, the sooner you will understand how to set all his captured ones free. They see the grand illusions he creates for them, but just like a spoiled child, Satan has little patience and if he doesn't get his way, he loses focus; makes mistakes. Now do you understand the clue of this dream?" the voice whispered.

Nodding again she was surprised when she heard a slight yes escape her mouth. The muzzle was gone.

"Ah she speaks at last, Satan said. So tell me Xian, just how do you think an insignificant human female can go up against me, ruler of this world and all in it?" he asked waving his hand over the blue orb below them.

"I don't. Actually I have no plans to go up against you at all."

"What? That's insane. Why would you then be called the Sword of Vengeance if not to be used against me? I am the only true opponent Father has."

"Not my business, but what is my business you better believe I plan on seeing it through to the end. Look it was an experience and all but I really need to go. Besides I got what I was brought here for, no need for me to soil myself with your company any further. I'll be sure to let Michael know you send him your love," she said as she felt herself falling back towards the planet below. Satan just stared at her in disbelief then she saw his fisted hands wave above his head and a loud scream rip from his lips.

"Xian, Xian, it's okay, it was just a dream," Michael's voice gently said as he pressed his head against hers.

Her eyes opened to see the top of his forehead. She reached up and ran her fingers through his shiny black hair. Closing her eyes again she exhaled a long breath. All she wanted to do was stay there next to this awesome man, angel, whatever.

"I'm sorry if I hurt you when I was all googled eye over him. I love only you, you know that right?"

Michael held up his head and looked at her. His eyes were the light blue that almost stopped her heart whenever she saw them. He nodded then pecked her on the lips. She smiled back at him then her face went serious.

"I saw him, he and I had a conversation of sorts. He mostly did the talking. I wasn't able to since a mysterious hand was covering my mouth. Anyways, I got the clues I needed and now I know how to save all the souls he's taken."

Michael didn't say anything, just nodded and rolled onto his back. He was happy to hear her confirm her love for him and that he had no need to think otherwise. He knew she was dreaming but wasn't sure what it was all about. All night she was tossing and moaning. He could only watch over her and stop her from rolling off the bed a few times. Not being able to go into the dream with her tore at him, but he knew The Father was with her which gave him a measure of peace. *So the real work begins*, he thought as he stared up at the ceiling.

Xian got out the bed with a burst of energy and turned on the shower so it could get nice and hot. Poking her head out the door she asked him,

"So are you going to just lie there, or get in here and take a shower with the love of your life?"

Before she could pull her head back into the bathroom he was naked at her side. She reached up and stroked the side of his face. Not sure where the sudden surge of energy and hope came from but she wasn't about to question it. Life was short enough and every moment she got a chance to make a difference in the life of someone else, she would do her best to take it. But for now, the only difference she wanted to make was in the life of the person wrapping her in his arms; the warrior angel who rescued her from self-denial, who directed her back towards her destiny, her embodied savior; Michael.

Satan searched every inch of the city for her from high above; nothing. *No way did she just disappear. She had to be somewhere down there!* he screamed in his head. Then as if on cue, Xian's face appeared before him. All she said was,

"Game on!"

Zita Grant is a freelance writer, author, avid reader, self-proclaimed movie critic and social media buff. Since her teenage years, she has been penning short stories and poems. Understanding the power a good story has, she works to create vivid experiences for those that venture into her tales.

Some of her passions include cooking, food tasting, reading, movies, gardening and traveling. Whenever she's not busy writing novels, or helping coach other writers, her time is spent enjoying the outdoors with friends and family. Keep up to date with Zita's latest offerings and events by connecting on Instagram and Twitter at @ZitaG_Author

Made in the USA
Middletown, DE
17 February 2018